U. 80

D1553912

The Antiphonary

The Antiphonary

Hubert Aquin
Translated by Alan Brown

Anansi/Toronto

THE ANTIPHONARY was published originally
by Le Cercle du Livre de France Limitée,
Montreal, Quebec

Cover design: Karen Loconte
Cover drawing: detail from Leonardo da Vinci's
                    The Sheet with Five Heads

House of Anansi Press Limited
35 Britain Street
Toronto, Canada

ISBN: 0-88784-426-X

Printed and bound in Canada by John Deyell Company

The one becomes two, the two becomes a three, and the three rediscovers unity in four.

(Axiom of Marie the Copt)

The Antiphonary

There is no pinning it down, nor knowing how it may unfold. Flaubert said as much. Others, among them Mahomet and doubtless Saint Paul, were also stricken by the frightful power of this event which is nowadays classed under the strange name of aura. The aura unfailingly precedes that hypersynchronic discharge known in former times as the ''mal sacré'' or falling sickness. Jean-William Forestier was threatened, this ninth day of his vacation with his wife in San Diego, and for the ninth time in his life, by just such an icto-comitial crisis, provoked — as Christine was by now well aware — by a manifest paroxystic bradycardia or, in nosological terms, the well-known Adam-Stokes syndrome.

After two vacation days in Santa Barbara, where Jean-William and Christine had driven in the superb Cutlass rented in Los Angeles, they had set off southward again, making their way as fancy led them through the endless sprawl of Los Angeles,

The Antiphonary

finding sun again at Santa Ana, then wheeling down the Pacific coastline to San Diego where they had arrived seven days ago. With these nine days behind them, dazzled by so much sun, befuddled by so much heat, they were no longer the pale city folk who had left Montreal in search of the peace and warmth unavailable in their boreal paradise in the month of March. Christine had been expecting the worst ever since they settled in at the Hillcrest Motel in San Diego: Jean-William was suspiciously relaxed. She observed him constantly and not without anxiety. She had, nonetheless, continued reading and making notes on her little in-folio by Jules-César Beausang, but her heart was not in it as before. Mechanically she poked away at a task which was in fact of the greatest interest and importance to her, for this was work preparatory to her projected thesis. On top of all this, the sun had been too much for her, and toward the end of the day she dozed off over her half-open book. Jean-William, for his part, was deeply tanned, and his blue eyes were more striking than ever in a face darkened by a surfeit of sun. Most of their days ended in a similar routine: after a meal of sea-food (usually), washed down with quantities of a California Chablis (from the cellars of Charles Krug, Napa Valley), they would go for a stroll along the beach and re-enter their motel quarters by the outside door numbered 138. Their room, in fact, faced north, and their window looked out on a parade of bays, peninsulas, necks of land, rocks and sharp escarpments, progressively softened and diluted by the distances of the California coast. At times Christine stared long at this unending landscape, a Leonardoesque perspective of beaches, meadows, inlets, amputated sea-arms and rocky cliffs: a vision of marvels that reminded her of Beausang's remarks on the optical theories of his contemporaries Vasari and da Vinci. Nature in those days had a quality of enchantment which it has lost, now that science has given currency to such terms as erosion, alluvial change, geodesic trans-

3

formations. Poor Beausang, thought Christine, he knew nothing of all that: he could not have made sense of the innumerable deltas of this plain that separates the sea from the Mojave desert, nor appreciated the spectacular beauty of Lower California. His world lacked this amplitude, and nature was stamped with the seal of the most perfect finality. Nature, for a man of his time, was bound to conform to the symbolic system so dear to the painters of the era. And yet for Christine the evidence that nature embodied no necessity, no coherence, no submission to divine or human ends, was there before her eyes: a flattened coast, a haphazard series of valleys, straits, table-lands, plains and gulfs, laid out in anarchy toward infinity.

"The earth is alive, like any living creature; it is a greater person, more vast than all God's other creatures," wrote Jules-César Beausang — typically — in his work, *De Natura Fossilium*, of which the national library in Montreal has a' thoroughly dog-eared first edition, a book that Christine had often held in her hands. This rare volume, published in Basel in 1531 when the author was only twenty-nine, was filled with the most outlandish analogies: the Earth, for Beausang, had hairs (plants and trees) and a voice (heard sometimes in the depths of caverns). The Earth could think; it sometimes even went so far as to sneeze ... These thoughts, set down by a Beausang or a Telesio, came back to her as she contemplated the raw haunch of the California coast, while her husband, Jean-William, took a hot bath to recover — at least so he put it — from certain discomforts which he was never quite able to discuss with his wife, but which had now set in toward dusk, after their meal, on this ninth day of their California holiday. Daylight was fading slowly, projecting elongated forms upon the sky; clouds, purple in the distance, were already dark nearby — an immense backdrop sliding imperceptibly toward the coming dark.

Christine knew well that Jean-William's "discomforts" were

merely premonitory signs of a sequence whose implacable course was quite familiar to her. Yet she lingered at the window, complacently regarding her own inner landscape and that other which spread its piebald beauty before her. Jean-William faded in her mind until he was as vague as the foothills of the Sierra Nevada: Christine had stopped thinking of the impending fit, of the hot bath in which Jean-William was immersed, even of the tragic situation in which she seemed inextricably caught. She had floated away. She too had her moments of absence, though they were nothing like Jean-William's. More and more often she found herself dreaming her way through this existence which should have commanded all her vigilance and awareness. Her mind wandered among the intricacies of Jules-César Beausang's thought, the confused theories of the alchemists, the lapidary of Scipio of Gabiano, the genders of stones (in which an observer of nature as great as Paracelsus had believed). A sound came from the bath.

She turned toward the bathroom door, suddenly conscious again, worried, uneasy ... Jean-William emerged naked and dripping wet. He staggered as if he had been drinking, then collapsed across the bed. Christine looked at him, went nearer: incredible! He was sleeping already, seemingly deep in a comatose abyss, as if under the effect of a strong anti-convulsive. Perhaps he was right in taking hot baths to overcome his suspect state of relaxation ... Christine was reassured. She covered him affectionately with a blanket so that he would not catch cold, took off her shoes and stretched out beside him. She picked up her Beausang and read, leaning against the head of the bed. The naive style of Beausang, "the 16th century Pliny," bordered at times on self-infatuation, for example when he strayed from the field of mineralogy and began aping the sort of writer who is attentive to his own 'self', attentive to the point of obsession with the slightest fluctuations of his own moods ... At such

5

times Christine felt a certain pity for the figure cut by this long-dead author. She had developed a weakness for this wretched man who, humiliated by his wife's infidelity, had left his native city (Ghent), his security, his children, to flee toward the south. Beausang had begun to keep a diary in the vernacular while he was in Basel. A strange man, Beausang, strange ... Christine thought she could never have loved such a man as that touchy individual, inclining to melancholy and pessimism, imagining that he was a detached observer of nature while in fact he ... Exhausted, saturated with sun, Christine fell softly asleep beside her husband.

Close by her side, Jean-William's deep breathing punctuated with its regular intervals the period of waiting which for Christine stretched into (and synchronously became) a long ribbon of boredom and desolation — one lone, interminable spiral, a vermicular entity whose slow, self-assured prehension was like a snake's. Repulsive images, they were the last in Christine's mind before her descent into exhaustion. Darkness had fallen on the foothills of the Sierra Nevada around the city; the sky, haunted by oblong forms, had turned to shadow for one night's duration. A deep night, soft, and almost hot ...

*   *   *

The eighth time, Jean-William had been struck down as if by lightning while the couple lay sound asleep in bed. Jean-William's cries, her spectral vertigoes, his terrors, his convulsions, his hallucinations, and finally his brutal fall to the floor, his stiffening into unconsciousness — Christine had forgotten nothing. She had finally called on Chilean neighbours (a consul or vice-consul newly arrived in the country) to help her move Jean-William's rigid body. The Chilean couple, in night-dress, had come along willingly, and both had helped Christine get Jean-William's body back on the bed. It had not been easy. Jean-William's stiffness had made things very awkward. After

6

this transport operation the couple in question — Suarez by name — had retired politely to their apartment next door. They had never brought the matter up again. Christine had mentioned it to Jean-William a few days later. This had been a mistake. Jean-William had reacted very badly to her revelation of the incident (rightly or wrongly, what was the difference!). He had considered the presence of the Suarez couple a humiliating intrusion, and as he had no recollection of losing consciousness he had trouble believing that the fit, this time, had left a gaping crater in his memory. His pride was wounded; he felt the integrity of his person retroactively diminished, reduced to the void that had replaced his field of consciousness during the time when his stiffened body lay on the bedroom floor.

Christine felt that Jean-William was wrong to take the incident as detracting from his personality. The Suarez couple were nothing to worry about, and in any case no humiliation could be associated with a pathological state. What could be a more obvious relic of the past than such a correlation, which would occur to no one nowadays! She should know about such things if anyone did, after two years' residence in several Montreal hospitals as a medical student. Again she had put her foot in it by mentioning her medical days, that period when Jean-William, who had worked nearby for a company located in St. James Street, did not yet know his future wife. Was it jealousy? Hard to say. Certainly he entertained confused and aggressive feelings towards the Christine who had been single at that time. And she had not even known him then! Of course she had done what so many other girls do when they are students of twenty-two or twenty-five. Nothing more, nothing special, nothing abnormal: she had lived freely, and freely made her discovery of life. Lovers, friends, infatuations, adventures that liberated more or less — everyday stuff it had been and still was. But Jean-William, abnormally vulnerable about such things, remained especially touchy on the

7

subject of amorous episodes in Christine's earlier life.

The eighth ... that was January ... and the next? The ninth? The question brought her wide awake. She suddenly realized that she had dropped off to sleep reading Beausang's book ... It had fallen from the bed along with a page of notes she used as bookmark. Beside her Jean-William slept a sleep that was infinitely profound, shaken at times by clonic tremors. She should get up, stay on the watch: Jean-William was, one way or another, approaching his ninth attack. A whitish froth emerged from his contorted lips; his whole body, shaken by charges of increasing power, showed that he was host to a tempest whose violence drained him of his being.

(Robert Bernatchez knew nothing of all this. He had loved Christine, but eleven years was a long time. Christine had married Jean-William, Robert had married Suzanne; and the past was the past, except at certain strange moments when Jean-William, derailed by one of his attacks, forced his wife to tell him everything, with full details and to the very end ... It was torture: intolerable, unbearable torture, exhausting for him and for Christine. They would both emerge from it shaken, bitter, disgusted with each other, defeated ...)

After a series of particularly violent spasms, Jean-William subsided into the apnoea of his crisis: pale, unconscious, he ceased breathing. Christine was all too familiar with the sinister sequence of the attack, with its transition from the tonic to the clonic phase, followed by that of apnoea, then on to the terrifying stage of stertorean breathing, the deathly rattling that generally precedes the end of the attack, and finally the hallucinatory delirium that follows it. Afterwards, lacunary amnesia is total: not a trace remains of what went on. Jean-William? Fresh as a rose, clear, transparent and devoid of memory as glass, purified of every blemish from the past. But sometimes this state did not last long.

The Antiphonary

Christine is thinking idly of Turin: she passed through there with Jean-William (two years ago, it was), but for her Turin is a desert where the disenchanted couple stopped overnight in a gloomy hotel. It was in July. In May she had given up medicine and a few days later had met Jean-William at a cocktail party where Robert, after a drink too many, had shocked her by his behaviour. But Turin, this time at one remove, brought back another memory: that of Jules-César Beausang, who sent his manuscript to a printer in Chivasso (close by Turin) to have it set and printed. And it is the whole story of this affair that he tells in his diary printed in Basel. Turin, terminal point in the troubled life of Jules-César Beausang, obsessive city haunting the thoughts of one who dreams she is a traveller, on foot.

The Antiphonary

Here begins the book I have pieced together from the documents
and fragments in my file. Without title, internal logic, content,
or any charm other than that of a kind of untidy truthfulness,
this book is composed in the form of an epileptic aura: it contains
the apparently innocent accumulation of a whole series of events
and shocks, the effect of life-weariness and its implacable manifestations. Nothing compelled me, nothing will ever compel anyone to write thus, in utter disorder, the kind of thing I am about
to write. Nothing is necessary; which is the same as saying that
everything, or almost everything, is aleatory. Jean-William's
ninth attack is barely underway and already I feel distant from
it, I am about to assume my distance from it, to find for it
an imaginary double, a kind of incommensurable temporal exten-
sion. I move coolly through a space-time whose borders are
difficult to discern: to be sure it begins with this bed in the
Hillcrest Motel in San Diego, but I tend less and less to see
myself beside Jean-William, who is pursuing without me his
epileptomorphic interlude, but Montreal emerges from the fog
(called smog in San Diego), Montreal where I lived too long
too badly, and then Basel, where Jules-César Beausang, a disciple
of Paracelsus, lived in exile; then Turin, and Chivasso on the
banks of the Sesia, an ancient village become a satellite-town
of Turin. And let us not even mention other cities where I burned
alive: Novara, Toulouse, Asbestos, Drummondville, Neuchâtel,
Geneva, Rolle, so many names without a history, so many fragments, greater and lesser mysteries, of the giant puzzle on which

The Antiphonary

I love to work in silence, far from those beds where the poor sick receive the first, annunciatory shocks in the clonic phase of the fit! Yes, far from that whole orgy of convulsions, spasms and raucous cries I move softly, I compose this book calmly, coldly, with no hallucinogen to drive me on, no hope to lead me astray, not even the (secret) hope of endowing it with the meaning and importance conceded willingly (by postulate) to books by authors who have achieved the slightest popularity. At first I felt a certain jubilation at preparing my PhD in science (subject: Medical Science in the XVIth Century); but that is all past now, I lost my thesis subject somewhere in the dunes of Santa Barbara and San Diego, my archei have drowned themselves in a comitial sea, my lower vena cava has overflowed into the Sesia, whence it became a tributary of the Ticino which, after flowing through Piacenza, Cremona, Ferrara, rushes immoderately into the Adriatic of Galen. Worse, I have wasted time, the years of my youth and the endless days I lived analyzing the splendid paradoxes of Theophrastus Bombast von Hohenheim and the multiple elucubrations of the Salernist scholiasts, not to mention the works of van Helmont and the treatises of Girolamo Fracastoro. Jean-Etienne de Calcar, patient sketcher of the countless autopsies of Vesalius, is my model: like him, I coldly sketch the intimate configurations I perceive through my lens. I am trying to compose this book as if it were a collection of illustrations — all of them treating one and the same strange, many-headed seizure, full of grace in its beginnings, spectral as it progresses, macabre in its conclusions, this very moment sucking at Jean-William's strength, and mine as I observe his terrible disorder.

At the start, when I began this thesis, I wanted to deal not only with the school of Salerno but also the "Averrhoist" centre in Padua; in addition I intended to include in my study a thorough commentary on the *De naturalium effectuum admirandorum causis sive de incantationibus* (generally known under the name

The Antiphonary

De incantationibus), by Pietro Pomponazi, a disciple of Alexander of Aphrodisia and, at one remove, of Aristotle, whom he wished to purge of his non-Aristotelian elements; I also intended a critical exegesis of the celebrated book of the no less celebrated Vanini, *De admirandis naturae reginae deaeque mortalium arcanis libri quatuor*. And with that I saw a still larger perspective opening before me, automatically including the "negative" dialectic (*via negativa*) of Nicholas of Cusa and the anti-Aristotelian system of Lorenzo della Valle . . . But finally I realized that I was really scattering my energies, wandering from this to that, simply to occupy my overheated mind: my passion for elaborate theories in fact disguised my search for something — anything — to keep me busy and allow me to forget the disaster that was my life. I had trouble accepting that I had given up medicine; and I suppose that I was really bored by the futile mazes of Cesalpino's epistemology. I made the mortal plunge into the famous *via negativa* of Nicholas of Cusa, without, however, emerging into the deist reward of his *coincidentia oppositorum*. Instead, I crawled within the *contractum absolutum* — a kind of infinite in the style of Duns Scotus, fond as he was of *subnotio* — as was Girolamo Fracastoro, for that matter. Decidedly, I was becoming "cephalophoric" like so many others; I was dissolving in the purgative emission of my own thought. The process was intoxicating, to be sure; this kind of stimulation was part of the game I was playing. I foresaw and even desired it with a recklessness that was typically Aphrodisian (the allusion is, of course, to Alexander of Aphrodisia), or else I moved within a pure "pharmacotriba" of the period. My dear reader, the "pharmacotriba" doesn't hold water any more. I yearn for some astrophilic sensation, some supersonic transfer, a burning that would cover me alive in flames and devil take the hindmost. This is indecent, beyond a doubt; but I prefer to reveal it with an anemophylactic passion. Here I am, you see, not naked or

The Antiphonary

natural (I believe less and less in human nature), but filled with Vesalian (or Vaselinizing) pharmacopias, smeared with radical "humid" liquid of the Averrhoist variety, pierced and leaking for all I'm worth, just as I am, just as I become, according to the orbital progressions of the divers cosmogonies whose imprint I recognize on my poor female body.

Had I known (in San Diego, while Jean-William was biting his tongue) what was to become of me afterwards, I would most likely have gone into hiding, in a grotto of San Mateo or San Rafael, and never again have reappeared under my own identity. A hippie on impulse, I would also have been a hippie incognito — covered with flowers green and yellow, rigged out like a fright, wandering in the swollen streets of San Francisco, never again to surface in Montreal . . .

But I had no idea, I knew very little, except that Jean-William Forestier, my husband (38 years of age, 152 pounds, five feet eleven, white Caucasian, born with a silver spoon in his mouth, a Jacksonian epileptic with gyratory Adam-Stokes syndrome, messed up like you wouldn't believe, practising Catholic) was twisting and turning in the unconscious irreversibility of his ninth symphony. I was almost kept awake by the rattle that came from his throat and the spasms that nudged me, but I had no inkling of the strange consequences of the events I intend to relate to you (without, in future, subjecting you to the self-indulgence of my fancier ideas).

I knew I should be helping him somehow, but I dozed off: the strong sunlight had impregnated my epidermis all day long, not without inducing a certain drowsiness. I was conscious; I was there, beside Jean-William, but his convulsions no longer shook me in an active way. Strange sensation. I flew from him at the same speed with which time (irretrievable as Horace said) fled on its way. My eyes were half-closed, I was dreaming, making up little stories in a depressant mode: there I was in

13

The Antiphonary

Basel in the form of Jules-César Beausang, a disciple of Vesalius, an unworthy but most sincere admirer of Paracelsus! "Nothing could be more lovely than the course of the Rhine through Basel: here the Rhine bears on its waves no burden but sadness and somber melancholy. How I wish that I could lose myself in its flood, as I look out upon it from number 9 Heintzerstrasse, where I have a lodging on the second floor ..." A minute description follows of his view of Basel from that balcony over the Rhine, and the river winding through the city. The ample windows are well described, and the style of Swiss houses of the late middle-ages: rich, quite comfortable, all windows in front, the facade jutting into the street and ending at the top in a curb-roof. Jules-César Beausang's further considerations are, moreover, such as to hold the attention of any reader. They are of all kinds and on all subjects, including Jules-César Beausang himself, whose person and history are far from lacking in interest for us in the 20th century. The manners of the citizens of Basel and the other Swiss cantons nearby are described in great detail, and the landscape is dwelt upon with rapture; but all this is overshadowed by the clinical observations made in passing on those patients treated by Doctor Jules-César Beausang, and the descriptions of himself, tired, depressed, filled with anxiety, then suddenly afflicted by an irregular but recurrent trembling of his lower limbs. My dream carries me off, I lose myself in Basel, in the meanderings of the Rhine, its density of sadness and its degrees of aqueous melancholy ... and all the while by my side Jean-William was swimming in another river, following other meanderings charged with meaning, other paths, other ways that were to lead him infallibly — or within certain limits of invariability — to the heart of his ninth attack (as yet unfinished!). How ungrateful I am to have left my course at this point to go wandering about in the insignificant dunes of my day-dream (or half-sleep)! But I know what I'm like, and this is a theme I'll return to, whether I like it or not; for this book I'm beginning is bound, in part at least, to reveal the woman who writes it.

Yes, I was staring vaguely at this man (Jean-William) sprawled on the bed right beside me, and I never gave a thought to the various ways in which medicine can cast out the epileptic evil — if there is sufficient warning, of course, But I was indifferent or (worse still) detached. Jean-William interested me not in the least. I even found him a bore with his everlasting shocks and tremblings and hyperventilated, raucous breathing. My head swam with all the myriad symptoms and syndromes that appear in this moment of incipient crisis; I suddenly found myself losing touch, drifting far from this wretched bed where my partner was puffing and blowing, to the oneiric regions I found so much more enticing than reality. The eighth time had come as a shock: the memory persists as a horrid nightmare. The snows of winter had wiped all the colour from Montreal, with no merciful shading: in my memory the scene was one great orgy of seminal white. (My half-dream was taking over my conscious mind . . .) The sinister white of Montreal on that January night was unforgettable: the conscious image I retained of it reminded me now not only of Beausang's *Principles*, in which the author shamelessly revives the hylozoist theory of Paracelsus, but also of that abominable night severed brusquely by a raucous cry from Jean-William and all the rest of it. He crumpled onto the hardwood floor with a muffled sound. I had just opened my eyes, barely opened them. I was not to close them again the rest of the night. I first tried to lift Jean-William, stretched at full length near the foot of the bed and rigid as a corpse. Failing in this, I went to the Suarez' door and knocked. They were our neighbours on that floor (I had never spoken to them). They were most helpful and came along, both of them, to help me get Jean-William back on the bed. Not until then did I realize that Jean-William was naked; but it was too late to slip anything on him, and could I have managed anyway? I lacked the needed *Wirkstoff* (dynamism) so dear to Philip Aurelius Bombast von Hohenheim. On the contrary, I was in a state of collapse, almost ashamed, incriminated by his very *sulfur vitrioli*. But Jean-William himself lay there in a coma, offering to the gaze of our neighbours his naked body and the obvious premonitory symptoms of his epileptic attack. The operation was an awkward one, for, stretched out rigid, Jean-William seemed to his bearers to be double his weight. The epileptogenic *esprit vital* had been turned loose on poor Jean-William and, in its blinding epiphany, had taken him over body and soul. The Suarez couple managed to lift the body, an immobile wife looking on in horror. All in all, it took about an hour. "Also gibt die Zeit auch den tugenden anderst und anderst ihre Krafft," as the author of the *Paragranum* would have said.

With the Suarez couple back in their apartment, I, the *wasserleuth* wife, simply resigned myself to waiting for the ninth attack; and, before that, to waiting for the sidereal dawn to seed the lining of our curtains. And in fact I did not close my eyes once. Driven to speculation, I speculated on my future, immediate and distant, utterly unpredictable.

The Antiphonary

If one were to attempt a resumé of the fundamental precepts formulated in his various works by Jules-César Beausang, one would have first to examine in some detail his conception (a new one at the time, i.e., in 1530) of the practice of medicine: he insisted strongly on the clinical aspect of medicine, on auscultation — as it is still practised — by percussion, as well as on a general examination of the patient. For, as he said, the illness of one part of a man can only be explained in terms of his general state. A major cause of the failures of Galenic medicine was ignorance of the *locus morbi,* J. C. Beausang maintained. It was thus important to study, not the anatomy of the body, but the body of the disease — and in this he followed what Paracelsus taught, that the anatomy of the time was a "dead anatomy." As we know, anatomy has been rejected by medical science for some centuries now because it teaches nothing but the static configuration of the interiors of dissected bodies, while disease is characterized by "anatomical modifications." Diseases — and Paracelsus professed this as well as Beausang — grow like trees or flames (*flammula*) in nature. The notion that disease has a life, even if that life verges upon agony and death, was thus postulated in the scientific thought of Beausang; and this postulate led to more rapid and efficient progress in pathology than all the axioms of Galen or Hippocrates or all the theories of humours or the mysteries of alchemy.

"All things," said Beausang, "must be put to the test of experience." Bombast von Hohenheim said: "*Erfahrung,*" and he said *"kunsthafft."* Van Halmont, for his part, spoke of *"wissen und erkantnuss,"* thus opposing clinical experimentation to pseudo-knowledge based on reason and the formal logic of Aristotle, Galen and Avicenna. Agrippa of Nettesheym summed up in a lapidary formula the difference between knowledge (according to the ancients) and exact knowledge obtained by the empiric method: "Nought but this union with the object gives man entry into knowledge, which is to say, the truth . . ." (in *BUCH VON DER GEBARUNG,* quoted by Huser, p. 118, Niieswurg, Leipzig, 1932).

Galileo and Copernicus, as everyone knows, later gave new impetus to the scientific movement by giving scientists of their day precise instruments with which to prospect reality. But in Beausang's day men of science tended to build rickety theoretical structures without the slightest empirical base. Girolamo Cardano, Nicholas of Cusa, Jules-César Beausang and Paracelsus were all contemporaries. Not to mention Patrizzi and Pomponazi. All these philosophers form the hinge between the Platonic revival and the discovery of the experimental method. And I have no scruple about including Jules-César Beausang as one of the clear-sighted precursors of the scientific movement of the Renaissance, despite a certain conceptual confusion typical of those great scholars who discovered the rudiments of strict scientific thought and the first instruments of modern medicine. Iatrochemistry and iatrophysics, practised in those days by J. C. Beausang and Vesalius, are modern therapeutic methods. In 1536 (just before his death) Jules-César Beausang was still fulminating against the "anatomist" methods of doctors who chained themselves to the dissection table: "The teaching of medicine, as it is practised today, with all the damage that is done by adherence to an insensate tradition, demands that an assistant devote himself exclusively to the dissection of the human body, while the professor, his nose buried in the manuals of Galen, reads aloud a completely

fanciful description of the different parts of the body exposed
by his assistant. He is enthroned all the while upon a podium
and confides to his audience those inviolable dogmas which he
has more or less by heart. And as the assistant knows no Latin,
and it is practically impossible for him to follow the pedant's
discourse, this stupid manner of teaching profits no one, and
all humanity continues to catch the Great Pox, firmly believing
that the absurdities of Galen and the aphorisms of Avicenna
will cure them." (From *Omnia Opera,* Basel, 1538). Some years
earlier Fracastoro had published in Venice his famous *DE
CONTAGIONE ET CONTAGIOSIS MORBIS,* an (anticipa-
tory) treatise on bacteriology in which the celebrated Italian doctor
describes the pandemia, most disturbing at the time, that syphilis
constituted, the *ophalim* of the Hebrews, the "French disease,"
as Paracelsus calls it. Anti-syphilitic remedies were a gold-mine
for quacks. Mercury ointment and Guaiacum made fortunes for
profiteers. Other treatments also enjoyed their vogue: ligature
and colostomy. Distinctions were made among bubonic syphilis,
visceral syphilis and another hereditary variety, all three being
scourges of God which, the Alchemists believed, transformed
the gout into gouty syphilis, paralysis into syphilitic paralysis,
ulcers into ulcerating syphilis etc. etc. etc.

When all is said and done I would be tempted to transform
my poor life into an epileptic paralysis, an ulcerating epilepsy,
a permanent and interminable Jacksonian crisis . . . or even into
a crititical Bravasian attack, luxury style without gyration. I do
not turn when I fall, but — wow! — I fall stupidly, without
warning, on tiles, in stairways, in San Diego and even on the
country road between Novara and Chivasso, that absolute city
(*citta absoluta*) toward which I plod, step by heavy step, humble
bearer of a precious manuscript accepted by me at the Swiss
border and awaited anxiously in Chivasso by the man who is
to print it (I mean the MS of the *Treatise on New Diseases*

by Jules-César Beausang). My name is Renata Belmissieri, Italian by birth, born in Cremona, beaten by my parents, wounded by life and earning a pittance by the smuggling of manuscripts forbidden by the King's censor in France ... I make my living from this strange contraband. It is, after all, no more degrading than haunting the streets of Turin after sundown or beating the sidewalks of Milan, that city of the damned, a thousand times damned, a city more libidinous than the most serene republic of Venice where I have never been. But a cousin who went there described to me that sordid, most serene republic, full of the stench, bearing off in the corrupt water of its canals the irreversible rot of its society.

The Antiphonary

Poor Renata Belmissieri, my double, the girl I use in the victim's role when I try, in projection, to imagine and depict a woman as subject to the recurrent spasms of the epileptic fit. She took delivery of a precious manuscript; and for this work she is well-paid. But the MS is contraband, and the risk is great. She picks up her package at San Bernardino, close to the Swiss border. She knows that she must take it to a printer called Carlo Zimara, number 6 in the Street of Santa Clara, Chivasso. She knows the way from San Bernardino to Novara and from Novara to Chivasso on the banks of the Sesia. It is not the first time she has smuggled manuscripts of one sort or another; she has already gone the route to Genoa or Turin, two cities that she knows like the back of her hand. This time she stops at Chivasso, just short of Turin. She knows nothing of the book she is carrying, not even the author's name, nor that of the person who brought the MS from Switzerland to San Bernardino. She knows only one thing: the name and address of the printer in Chivasso. She left San Bernardino at dawn, hiding the manuscript under her skirt. Then, tired of walking slowly because of this obstacle, she concealed it under a mass of herbs, and so was able to carry it more easily and at a better pace. She knew that in any case she could not reach Chivasso before night.

Toward sundown she found a quiet grove just off the Turin road. She took refuge there to sleep, for she knew that it was unwise to travel at night. When she had reached this dark and tranquil retreat she stretched out in the grass, as she had lain

21

in the hay when she was a child. The hunger she had felt before she reached the grove had now disappeared, and she was quickly overtaken by a heavy sleep. She fell swiftly into a profound trance. When she became conscious again it was not yet dawn. She was in complete darkness; but the shocks had already begun to descend through her body. This intimate terror was familiar to her. She well knew the mode of its appearance and the frightful sequence it would follow. Her parents in Cremona had come upon her one day in the midst of such an attack. They thought her possessed by the devil. She had fled then from her family home, as soon as she was physically able, for she suspected her parents of intending to shut her up in the Bergamo asylum, an institution whose reputation for horror was well-established. So, she had fled; she stole a fruit or a tomato here and there to keep herself alive. In Turin she had succeeded in passing for a widow — that is, a respectable person — but at 27 this was not easy. All the men wanted to marry her, believing her normal and endowed with the inheritance of which she boasted. She had finally changed cities, passing from Turin to Genoa, and changed identities, pretending to be the faithful spouse of a soldier in the Royal Guard. And that had worked. She had supported herself, living in a priest's house and doing his house-keeping, confessing more often than was normal, but never admit-ting to anyone that she was ill, that she had fits of trembling. When she felt one coming on (and she prayed to God that it would not happen in the street!), she made the excuse of nausea caused by pregnancy ... After a certain time the priest, with some temerity, established the fact that she had a very flat belly for a woman two months gone. Next day she fled again, only to begin with the same strategem in a parish outside Genoa. This time she was armed against surprise and simulated a more plausible belly, padding it progressively. Then the whole process started elsewhere a few weeks later. It was in one of these relatively lively periods (for she had to go to market in town every morning) that she had made the acquaintance of another priest's housekeeper who slyly intimated that she could make her belly larger or smaller at will. Surprised, Renata reacted badly to a remark she took to be personal, for it was made with a smile. But the other, a girl her own age, did have a swollen belly, and that fascinated Renata. She was not sure whether she was being exposed, or whether the other, by finding her out, was in fact revealing herself to Renata ... The two young women smiled at each other and walked part of their way together carrying provisions for their masters.

"You too? ..."

But Renata was still not sure. She hesitated to speak frankly.

"All right," she said at last. "Me too ..."

The two girls burst out laughing, and laughed a long time together. They went on walking, and people turned to look.

"Come with me," said the other.

And Renata let herself be drawn into a little lane. The other, called Rosalita, said she had fooled three priests round about Parma with her false belly, so as to earn an easy living after running away from her family in Livorno. But this time she was afraid that she really was pregnant by the priest who was sheltering her ... And she did not know what to do. A friend from her home town, who had run away to hide an illegitimate childbirth, had found a better system. She had become a smuggler between Switzerland and Italy, saying she was the wife of a soldier killed in combat. Smuggling, it seemed, was the thing in the North, a good living for girls with no home and no identity. Renata was especially interested in her companion's story for she knew that her own system could not work indefinitely.

"But do you know people I can trust, to get me in this smuggling business from Switzerland to Italy?"

"Yes," said Rosalita. "A printer in Chivasso, called Zimara.

The Antiphonary

But you must take care, for he buys forbidden books. So you work through a priest in Turin: the abbot Leonico Chigi, of San Tomaso parish ... ''

And the girl called Rosalita had explained to her the shortest way to walk to San Tomaso in Turin. Their chatter turned to the many similarities in their lives, these almost parallel lives of two girls banished by their respective families. Then, Rosalita's good advice to Renata: she exhorted her not to run away with the provisions she had bought for the priest, for that was too flagrant, too serious a crime. She would be better to leave at dawn and tell her priest she was off to visit a cousin who was a nun in the convent on the edge of town.

Renata took her advice. That evening she stayed like a good girl in the little attic room from which she often looked out at the city lights. She daydreamed about the new life she was about to begin next morning in the small hours. Already she began to miss her little room in the priest's house, with its illusion of comfort and security, its atmosphere of warmth, of generosity and respect ... Rosalita was a smart girl. Renata reached the point of wondering if maybe Rosalita really was pregnant by the priest she worked for. That presupposed a degree of corruption the very thought of which made Renata shudder. She would never have imagined a priest doing that in the secrecy of his presbytery. She, Renata, had been lucky not to meet that kind of priest, for indeed it would be all too easy, the trap was a yawning one ... She went to sleep very late, and the sky of Genoa was struck with luminous stars on a field of blue, her notion of holy infinity ...

Next day, at about five-thirty in the morning, while the sun rose, she knelt before her venerable priest to ask a dispensation of one day to go visit her cousin, the nun, who now lived in a convent close to Genoa. The priest said yes. And Renata, deeply moved, left on the strength of her lie.

The Antiphonary

The abbot Chigi was impeccably polite and distant. He gave Renata Belmissieri all she needed: passwords, tricks to foil customs agents, ways to communicate with Carlo Zimara (the printer); and, finally, his benediction. Doubtless moved by her answers to his questions about her strange malady, he kissed her affectionately on both cheeks and sent her on her way. She was to sleep on his duty cot in the Turin presbytery until daybreak. What was more, he tactfully slipped her four crumpled banknotes to pay for food, drink or lodging. After this brief meeting he withdrew to a carved wood confessional. She lay down on the priest's uncomfortable bed.

San Bernardino is two days' walk from Turin, in the precipitous mountains near Como, not far from Lugano. She arrived late, toward eight in the evening, in this little mountain village touching the Swiss border, and went straight to the Mountain Inn as the abbé Chigi had directed. It was a modest little hostel, bare of comfort, frequented by seasoned travellers and pilgrims crossing the Alps on their way to Rome. Renata was exhausted when she arrived. She collapsed on the bed in the room numbered 17 to which she was shown. In that moment she was filled with dread that her abominable illness would appear again, descending like a plague on her frail body. The deep sleep into which she fell was her protection for a time. Next day, as arranged, an old, white-bearded man (who spoke no Italian) came to her as she was eating her scanty meal in the main room of the inn. He seemed circumspect, took his place at a neighbouring table and said nothing. Renata was impressed by him. She did not know what to do, and wondered with some anxiety if he were indeed "the one". In fact, he waited a good while, then, having stared at her long enough, left her a well-tied parcel (a heavy old thing, Renata thought to herself), smiled, and went his way without more ado. On the parcel a curlicued address was written in ink: "Carlo Zimara, printer, Chivasso, by the usual way." In a moment Renata had concealed the parcel under her voluminous linen skirt. Then with her booty she was on her way to Chivasso which is not far from Turin on the north shore of the Sesia, a leaping river that runs down the Alps to the Ticino in a winding succession of cascades and rapids. Renata strode happily along by this pretty river, bordered by trees of all sorts, on a little country road that was to lead her to Chivasso. The heat of early afternoon had passed and Renata was still walking at a good pace. On the way she had met a few peasants and country women who greeted her with a wave. Renata was pleased by this border country, which she had never visited before. As she walked she discovered the landscape with a kind of elation, these trees, the river, the sky bounded on the north by a ribbon of unfamiliar mountains: the Alps, a rolling canvas background going from Monte Ceniso to Monte Cuneo ... Her career as smuggler seemed much more attractive than living out a lie that could be exposed any week by an unexpected epileptic attack.

It had been a nuisance, too, having to invent a whole series of stories about the comings and goings of her non-existent husband, that soldier in the Royal Guard. Renata was depressed by all these implausibilities; she was burdened by them, and in the end (because of her concern for truth) she was more affected by her fate as a fictitious wife than by her real misfortunes as a banished daughter.

* * *

That evening she found a quiet grove, a little dark for her

26

taste but — she told herself — sweetly restful: she hid there and settled down for the night, for she would be obliged to spend at least one night in the open before reaching Chivasso. She lay in the tall grass at the edge of the grove, and went quickly to sleep, exhausted by her long tramp from San Bernardino. When she awoke, before dawn, she was prey to the worst spasms that had ever shaken her body. In electrifying waves, she trembled. Her whole body was shocked at once, straightening and curling like a whip. She knew all too well this abominable distress, this sinister isolation, this most frightful of all sensations: the certain onset of a fit of possession (perhaps madness). The sky lit up above the trees, and the seizure, which had begun before daybreak, continued to run its implacable course. Renata hoped only that no one would pass nearby at that moment, to notify the police of the village and throw her in prison. She felt an indefinable terror. She expected the worst, weeping softly, but did not know what the worst might be. She had been sure she would pass out at one point, but it did not happen. She had the sense of having retained consciousness through the whole course of her attack ... Was this an illusion? Difficult to say. Renata remained there, propping herself against a tree, softly weeping over this nameless evil that degraded her. She kept waiting for the signs that the attack was over, but they were not much in evidence. On the contrary: she feared that the spasms would be renewed if she set out on her way, and saw herself falling in a faint on the road to Chivasso or God knows where.

Finally, collecting all her courage, she stood up. She took a few weak and timid steps, exhausted and above all fearful ... But she lay down again, not knowing if she was still too feeble or if her dizziness was a vestige of the attack. But the day was getting on (she had probably slept a few hours without knowing it), and she must, she thought, get up the spirit and energy to press on to that village near Turin, Chivasso, and deliver the manuscript she had carried clandestinely from the border. Then the printer whose name was marked on the package would give her a handsome reward for her trouble. In fact, that would be her due payment, quite simply, for the successful transport of the book. But since she had fled her family in Cremona, Renata lived in a threatening world, and she could never reason coldly about pay received for services gladly rendered. Her guilt would not leave her, and she had a groundless fear of some day coming face to face with her father or mother. This was an obsession, and the very notion of it kept her from acting in a normal way and deprived her of any sense of security in her dealings with others.

Poor Renata ... Before her eyes she had a copy of the MS of Jules-César Beausang: the *Treatise on New Diseases*, by Jules-César Beausang, chemist and philosopher. She could have read certain passages of the famous "Description of Epilepsy". Poor Renata — "a pitiable human struck by epilepsy, the body trembling as if heaven and earth were moved by the storm. The bladder often leaks. Convulsions are caused by this discordant tempest, producing occlusion of the eyes and inflammation of all the limbs. The disease disjoints the limbs, and weakens or breaks them, as is well known. All this goes on within the man, inside him. Then comes the supreme suffering, wiping out consciousness and penetrating to the very centre of his being ... " (Published by Boudon, Paris, 1901, Vol. XI of the *Complete Works*). Renata could have had access to the more or less precise ideas of Jules-César Beausang; she could have reflected on the scholarly transposition of what she knew too well from experience. And if she were led thus to new depths of disillusion, Renata, poor little smuggler, might have found some satisfaction in the nosological despair of the celebrated XVIth century physician who concluded thus: "Take pity, then, on those patients attacked by the falling sickness and pray God that a swift death deliver them

The Antiphonary

from the unbearable existence they must lead." (*Idem*) Poor Renata! And poor century, in which the sick were condemned to the worst catastrophes of life, or (worse) to the atrocious medical treatment of that age. When I began my thesis on this subject I never imagined I would make such horrifying, stupefying discoveries. Compared with the medical books of a man like Beausang, or Fracastoro, the descriptions of crimes perpetrated against the *Untermenschen* in Nazi camps makes pleasant bedtime reading.

As I try to put these thoughts on paper I can see through our window how the California sky takes on its shifting colours and darkens for (I was going to say "for ever") for the space of a night. Jean-William finds me a little manic. He says I have ants in my pants, I always have to be doing something. If tomorrow he sees these lines that I've written on hotel notepaper, which I found in the drawer of the single commode in our room, he will swear it's a love-letter secretly intended for someone else. It's always the same: he suspects me — you might say with glee — of every imaginable kind of desire, and a measureless capacity for libidinous intentions directed at people other than himself. The truth is much less amusing, for these famous lusts and hedonist intentions of mine are directed towards him, no one but him ... The page I have just begun has caught my fancy, but I can not predict in advance that it will make any sense at ...

The Antiphonary

It happened like this. I was staring at the wide-screen landscape before me (and perhaps dozing off), when I received a blow from a fist, full-force, on my temple. My head knocked against the lampshade, and the lamp fell with me. On the rug, half-conscious, I lay on my back. Probably a few seconds passed before I opened my eyes, but in that instant a kick made me cry out with pain, in a kind of groan, and I twisted to protect myself. His fits had never taken on this percussive violence. To be sure, in the apartment in the rue Grenet ... but a second hail of blows prevented me from lingering over that memory. Jean-William had indeed grown madly aggressive toward me, at the height of his attack. He was trying to kill me, destroy me, break every bone in my body. On all fours, overwhelmed, groaning and whining, I inspired no pity whatever in him. He went at me with his feet in a mad fury. I had the awful feeling, with each kick I received, that another rib was breaking, and — sordid but true — I was scared stiff. I could expect anything from this new-found enemy who had erupted against me with sudden, incredible rage.

I thought he would kill me. I had never been so terrified. And never had my fear been so justified as by the horrors that were now aimed at me, innocent though I was. Crawling on all fours, I succeeded in hiding behind the back of the black armchair (the one on the left, near the bed) where I was for the moment sheltered from Jean-William's uncoordinated blows. This respite allowed me to gather my wits a little, and also

The Antiphonary

to reflect on my panic. I had a glimpse of Jean-William, out of breath, crashing across the foot of the bed, either from vertigo or general exhaustion. His eyes rolled upward and his breath came fast, almost gasping. He seemed to be at the peak of his attack, perhaps approaching the clonic phase. Strangely enough, I no longer felt anything for him. He horrified me, that was all. And, to be honest, I would gladly have been rid of him that very moment. In my inmost heart I was scandalized by this damned illness which once again had assumed the obscene, animal aspect of a storm of violence directed against me. With an effort I stood up, clinging to the back of the chair that had been shielding me. I knew only one thing: I wanted to get away, get outside, take off in the rented car and let him die in that horrible motel in San Diego. As I stood up I had the hateful sensation of being dislocated and wounded in every part, teetering, on the point of vomiting (with no reason); and I staggered a few steps toward the commode. I had to be fast, for if Jean-William in his murderous madness saw me trying to escape he would be capable of anything. I took my handbag (I had some money at least) and took one last look at his body lying across the foot of the bed in a posture of absolute exhaustion. I had already reached the door. But what did I see? Jean-William was watching me with an expression of unbearable intensity. Was he even conscious? I should not have taken the time to ask myself the question. An ashtray (very heavy) crashed above my head, showering my hair with a thousand splinters. I managed to open the door just in time to avoid any further destructive enterprise against my person. Tough luck on my dear husband, said I, slamming the door (once I was outside and safe from blows).

In the apartment on the rue Grenet — I think it was the seventh attack — his rage had been less frightening. That time I lost no more than a dress, a few toilet articles and a certain degree of confidence in Jean-William. It's true I had a great bruise

31

on my hip, which even made me limp a little. But Jean-William had stopped of his own accord — in the middle of his fit, if I remember rightly — and fallen unconscious for a good ten minutes. I had had time (with the reflex of a practising doctor) to prepare a shot of Demerol and inject it in his shoulder before he came to. Thus I had had plenty of time to calm myself, size up the damage done and even phone Lecavalier's pharmacy and order some liquid largactyl. But in San Diego things were different for both of us. In the first place, Jean-William had not seemed inclined to violence before he attacked me; and I myself must have been a little muddled or I would have been sharper in observing the critical development of the comitial attack. And when I received that first blow on my temple I was wool-gathering about Beausang (sad in his room, in Basel) and Renata, young Italian smuggler-girl hidden in the high grasses of the grove where she had slept, terrorized by recurrent spasms of generalized flexion (Bravais-Jacksonian). But at her side she had the pre-Jacksonian descriptions by Beausang which, after all, included a number of different kinds of seizure: the procursive, the temporal, the partial but continuous, the myoclonic (which Rabot thought he was discovering in 1899!). Yes, I was lost in my reverie, absent, happy in my imaginary exile into history, when Jean-William's hard, closed fist came down on the upper left temporal lobe of my poor head. And it didn't stop there. Kicks were to follow blows, and I was to end up, unpredictably, on all fours behind the back of the black armchair (left of the bed), peeking out at the closed eyelids of this mad adversary who had inflicted such humiliation on me that I even (very briefly of course) considered killing him. Instead I ran away from this man I had married for better —as the formula goes — or for worse. In this case it was the for worse that I had to confront, after the first 15 years without violence — fifteen years of for better.

The Antiphonary

I began this book for no reason on the beach at Santa Barbara, as a narrative of events. Then life forced its way into my poor diary and transformed it into an autobiography. And here I am exhibited in broad daylight, poor fool that I am, bare to the waist, topless, breasts in the fresh air and soul discomfited. After all, who would refuse to the author of this book (myself!) the right to exhibit herself with not the slightest redeeming factors, with no euphemisms, no desire to make the couple look better than it was? No one (I make the choral response)! The couple (that fragile mini-society which procreates and does other odd things when the man and woman are not at each other's throats the whole day long in a single-family dwelling) is only one of the senseless modalities of life in common. I venture to believe that the time is past, and long past, when one was obliged to sing the praises of home life and the virtues of the wife who waits like Penelope for her sailor husband to come from his shitty little Homeric singsongs. Homeric days are over. The new era is here and God knows the new era will be new with a vengeance . . .

I had a future as a doctor. Everyone knows, by the way, that the word doctoress is just not used, when we mean a female doctor. But at 37 (having at 26 left my practice in its cradle) I have no future, as doctor or as woman, for I am disenchanted. I'm told I can always write. But I have things to say about the literary vocation that are perhaps in doubtful taste. Never mind, if I hadn't received on the left temporal bone a certain blow from Jean-William's fist I would not be sitting here trying to forge phrases that fumble at my brassiere and expose to the view of maniacs the slightly discoloured skin of my two breasts. I say "discoloured," though it happens that my breasts are notable, if I may say so, for their whiteness. Apart from a few rare, immodest exposures to the sun, that part of my body has always remained veiled by the chaste apparel of the young girl

The Antiphonary

I was and the young woman I am ceasing now to be. You may
say that at 37 one does not give up all hope of feminine fulfillment,
one does not renounce the complete and satisfying life that nowadays is the right of women. True! But you, dear female readers,
misunderstand me because you have not experienced half of what
I have been through in my poor existence, you have not been
once around my garden, nor, as in my case, accumulated such
a store of surprises and orgasms that future joys are no longer
exciting or capable of giving back the youth I wasted in probing
the bottomless theories of Simon Stévin, William Harvey, Sebastian Franck, Marsilio Ficino and Marçile d'Enghien — practising
to the death and to my own loss my *québecoise* version of the
forma specularis . . .

One blow from a fist knocked the learned theories sideways,
believe me. Having slammed the motel door behind me (what
luck!) I somehow struggled to where the Cutlass was parked,
the "burnt sienna" Cutlass we had rented in Los Angeles. I
drove off in a whirlwind and, not sure where to go, I came
out on a dark street which ended at the unlit beach. Here I
cut the motor so as not to stir up too much sand. There was
no one on the beach. The Pacific surf drummed at the night
with its heavy rhythm. I stumbled in the sand, my hair flying
in the sea-wind. There was no one, no light to be seen anywhere.
I was alone, marvellously alone, and (beyond doubt) past the
reach of the blows of that sick, convulsive creature who had
struck me in a way that was quite inadmissable. Tripping over
something in the sand of the dunes, I fell full-length, face down.
My face began (right then, it seemed) to hurt atrociously; but
nothing in that total dark reflected my image and I had no notion
of the extent to which I was unilaterally damaged. I knew that
it was near the left superciliary ridge, but I could not be more
precise. The pain was terribly piercing but in one respect at
least I was lucky: as I rose to my feet again on that uneven

34

The Antiphonary

ground I was sure I had no fractured bones . . . I had left on the headlights of the rented burnt-sienna Cutlass ('69 model). They projected a ghostly glow toward the darkened ocean. I began to feel better about things. The fresh new wind that was coming from the open sea had invigorated me. I decided to proceed with my flight from San Diego, a city forever ruined for me. And Jean-William must at that moment still be stretched upon the bed, powerless, perhaps not yet conscious. It was surely best to get away while it was still dark. I went back to the car and by dint of some manoeuvering managed to extricate it from the sand, not an easy feat; but finally, and after much effort, I turned onto a bit of road that led to a lamplit street in San Diego, Ocean Park Avenue, lined with rich villas. All the houses were surrounded by open fences and tall palms that swayed in the Pacific breeze. At the end of Ocean Park Avenue there was a shopping centre with brightly-lit windows. I pulled up by the sidewalk. And at last I saw myself in the rear-view mirror of the Cutlass: I was horrified. I looked like a harridan fresh from a brawl with the Mafia. The ridge of my brow was bleeding, I could see the open split from which the blood welled. And my left temple was abnormally swollen, not to mention the fact that the bridge of my nose (between the eyes) had an inexplicable cut, as if Jean-William had sawed at it. Mascara was running down from my eyes, making me look even more hideous. I lay sideways on the front seat of the Cutlass, shaken now by a flood of irrepressible tears. My face was wounded, and so was my body (that was not to be seen in the rear-view mirror of the Cutlass, but I knew it). Despair — there is no other word to describe my state of mind — wiped me out. I had lost all hope of a decent life, of regaining my face and body as they had been. Filthy, monstrous, I lay there on the seat and wept, incapable even of fleeing San Diego. I had no energy for it, nor any desire. Jean-William must have been truly

35

mad, completely altered, to have struck me as he had done just now. Horrible, yes, like a nightmare, unbelievable, the very idea of it set me off in tears again. I was weeping for myself, but also for our love; it's not funny to have wrecked your life and discover the fact at 37 when everything is beyond repair and ruined forever! And it's not funny to lie groaning like a poor idiot on a car seat in a completely strange city, San Diego. The world had crumbled along with my facial charms, my young wife's face. I was in despair, powerless, fed-up with life, discouraged ... Yes, suicide, I thought of it, I thought of it the whole time as I mourned over my personal life (a failure) and my lost love ... Then suddenly — in the midst of racking sobs — I had one thought — one last thought — for Jean-William, poor epileptic I had loved and from whom I had wanted a child (luckily tomorrow or even tonight my period was due). So much for the good life, so much for my hopes of a child from a man capable of killing me in a fit of epilepsy or kicking me in the face until he was tired. Poor Jean-William, poor Renata Belmissieri about whom I'd been thinking at the hotel, poor husband that I had to go and choose (and that's a stupid thing to say, I don't really hold a grudge against him). It's not really his fault, after all; and tomorrow if I'm not beside him on the beach he will understand that I've run away, but he won't be able to recall the scene of his violence, when he struck me down, beat me, kicked me ... Poor man ... I remember after his seizure in the rue Grenet apartment he had a case of amnesia that most people wouldn't believe. When at last he'd become aware of me, bruised, ruined and limping, with my dress all torn, he began to ask my pardon. It was almost touching; yes, it was touching! There I was, reassuring him about things he'd done to me which he had completely forgotten. That time he had wanted to kill himself. He repeated over and over that he didn't want to live with such a frightful disease.

The Antiphonary

In my rented burnt-sienna Cutlass, parked any old way at an angle to the curb, I suddenly felt how odd and suspicious I must look in the eyes of any citizen in the least concerned about law and order in the streets of San Diego. If I were noticed (it was late in the evening, though still not ten o'clock) by a passerby, he would certainly think he was doing the right thing in calling the San Diego police, and what could I say to the police?

Fear of this made me start the car again and drive around at random in the streets of San Diego, fast enough, of course, so that pedestrians could not see my swollen face. Neon signs, store windows and street lamps drifted by; I had been driving for some time, but I felt that my behaviour was not too rational. It was even illogical; yet, if I went back to the motel what would become of me? I discovered an immense shopping-centre in the heart of San Diego and it occurred to me that I would be less noticeable there. I parked the car not far from the stores and turned off the key. Again I looked in the mirror: I was horrified. My face bore marks that were not easy to camouflage. Then I remembered the glove compartment. Incredible, there they were! I had forgotten a pair of sun-glasses in it some days ago. I took them out (I had since bought a second pair after getting these in Santa Barbara) and put them on. If I veiled part of my face with scarf I had bought during our trip to Italy I could move about without attracting too much attention. At least, so I thought. And right in front of me was a drugstore (with a cosmetics counter) where I had already decided to buy a selection of foundation creams and powders, plus tweezers and pale lipstick, very pale, skin-colour. And also a little soporific and analgesic (acetylsalicylic acid) for I needed not only to disguise my wounds, but also to spend a night or two resting from my attack. The moment I left the Cutlass I saw a clerk leave the drugstore and disappear into an old Chevrolet where her fiancé or husband

37

was no doubt waiting for her. In the back of the store (the drug-store) the druggist (recognizable by his white smock) was counting the day's cash. He was emptying the cash-drawer and writing figures on a piece of paper. It's now or never, I thought, he'll be closing any minute. I left the car and walked, despite the shooting pains I was now experiencing, toward the pharmacy door. I pushed one of the aluminum-framed swing doors. A soft buzzer sounded at once. Poor Renata, poor me as well, lost here in San Diego, while Renata, all trembling, tried to go on to Chivasso and make herself known to the printer Carlo Zimara. Renata, carrier of the MS of Jules-César Beausang. The pharmacist of San Diego, seeing his client, made a movement in her direction.

"Car accident?" he asked.

I nodded, my face swollen and covered with blood and water (it mixed with the tears I continued, despite myself, to shed).

"I'll call a doctor," he said, having seated me in an armchair. He seemed worried, even panicked . . .

But I said in my best English, "Never mind calling a doctor. I am a doctor. Yes, I have a medicine degree from Montreal. Please do not call on another doctor, please. I will tell you what it is all about. There is nothing to worry, please."

The druggist looked at me long and incredulously. But he did not make the call — luckily for me.

"Just hand me a prescription tablet and a pen. I will make a prescription, OK?"

"What kind of prescription?"

"Liquid Demerol 500 mg," I said. "Let us say ten or twelve ampules — a box, a container . . . you know?"

The druggist smiled at me, with a kind of tenderness, for the first time. He understood that I had been beaten up, but could he guess that my own husband had done it? . . .

The Antiphonary

Now Renata rose from the corner of the grove where she had lain the night through. She had tried several times to walk, then sat down in the grass, weak and sweating. After a few equally fruitless attempts she managed to set out again for Chivasso. She has hours of walking ahead of her, and the heat is overpowering. But this book she is carrying fills her with the compulsive sense of implacable mission. She cannot throw it into the Sesia, whose impetuous stream tumbles along beside the road. She has no right to wander off, cheating time, beneath some comfortable haycock. Somewhere the author is waiting impatiently for his book to be published at last! The printer too is waiting.

The Antiphonary

But in these hours that passed so slowly for Renata Belmissieri she could not know that the author in person (a fact with which I am acquainted, as I have read a good many books about the sixteenth century) had left Basel for the south, uneasy over the fate of his manuscript. In Kloten a band of ruffians fell upon him and stripped him of all save a few reams of paper he kept to jot down his thoughts. It is through his own account, which survived him, that I, Christine Forestier, know all these things. Penniless, poor Beausang somehow arrived on foot in Bienne, where he found a helpful physician (his name is unknown to me) who believed the whole story: Beausang's exile from Basel, the robbers' attack, the theft etc. (*vide* Beausang's book). Beausang quickly persuaded his excellent colleague to let him earn a little by practising under him. Thus Beausang worked for a while in the practice of the physician of Bienne. He spent many hours visiting the surrounding countryside observing the manners of the peasants, inhabitants of Bienne who spoke Schwytzerdeutsch. From Beausang we can acquire all kinds of precise information about Bienne and its surroundings: that the husbands of the region beat their wives, that the configuration of their farm buildings was thus or so, that there were such and such peculiarities in the climate. It would seem that time was of no great importance to him at this stage in his life, for he did not note exactly the duration of his stay in the area. But certain other details are revealed to us: for example, his departure from Neuchâtel and what happened afterwards. In fact

The Antiphonary

Jules-César Beausang seems to have taken illegal possession (stolen is too discordant a word) of certain securities and cash, for he never again had money problems. The excellent colleague who had taken pity on him failed, perhaps, to notice his loss at once. But Beausang's theft can have been no petty one, for on his arrival at Neuchâtel he was able to buy a fine wardrobe and pass for an ambassador of the Republic of Venice, a sharp piece of knavery that allowed him to pass through Customs in every Protestant canton without opening a piece of baggage (and God knows there were customs-posts enough between Neuchâtel and Turin, the latter located in the kingdom of Piedmont)! But Jules-César Beausang travelled all the way with impunity, disguised as His Excellency, paying, no doubt, sizable tips to the porters of his trunks laded with stolen goods. He crossed the Alps by the route most frequented at that time, the Simplon Pass, passing through Brig, Domodossola, Locarno, Stressa, Borgomanero (in the Italy of our time). On the Italian side this road follows the course of the Sesia after Borgomanero and at several points coincides with the old country road which Renata Belmissieri took before she stopped to sleep in a grove of trees not far from the road, and which she followed the next day to reach Chivasso. But she was quite unaware that she was the bearer of a manuscript by a famous man who had, moreover, passed himself off for another famous man during this long voyage over the barrier of the high Alps. The traveller disguised as ambassador, for his part, knew nothing of Renata Belmissieri and the epileptic fits that were the bane of her life. He knew nothing, for he travelled in a heavy coach and was somewhere ahead of the poor girl who struggled on despite her empty stomach and attacks of nausea, not to mention dizzy spells and visions of luminous filaments of all possible colours in the sky above her (a kind of visual hallucination fairly common in the post-paroxystic manifestations of the falling sickness). He did not

know (and no more did she) that the author of this book, the
famous Doctor Jules-César Beausang, would arrive just a few
hours before the girl in the Piedmontese village of Chivasso.
From that moment on, this odd de-synchronization was to create
a dramatic situation in which these two persons (Jules-César
Beausang and Renata Belmissieri) would be strangely entangled.
If I know these things, it is of course because my vantage point
in time has allowed me to read the diary of the famous doctor
in its first version edited by the Turin priest, the abbot Leonico
Chigi. This edition, often reprinted, also contains a number of
fascinating revelations of the ideological attitudes current among
the Italian clergy of the period. But I have some way to go
still, and certain incidents to relate, before I come to tell you
what I think in my heart of hearts about Christian virtue as practised by the beloved clergy in those days, every single cleric
more monstrous than the next, more impious and heretical than
all the rest. And if I have time I will impart to you certain
secondary considerations on the substantial and eternal second-
class condition of woman from the XVIth century to our own
time. It is really very amusing, simply marvellous and irresistible.
(As feminism is in a bad way these days I feel that I am losing
more and more women readers. Too bad, but that's how it goes).
Where was I? Let me get back to minding my sheep (another
second-class species which I hereby invoke in a process of benefi-
cent transfer). I am tired, stupidly tired after this incredible
‘‘beaten woman’’ act — I mean my own — in San Diego, at
the Hillcrest, just two days ago. Two days have not been enough
for the contusions to·cauterize and the hematic damage to be
repaired, but the bruises (on my face, on my belly, on my arms)
have had ample time to turn from blue to a violet-yellow-crimson,
a kind of multicolour rainbow on a living screen (as in the invention of the famous Ian Tired). I have the unpleasant feeling,
when I make the slightest move, that the various parts of my

poor body are dislocated, detached from one another, no longer
forming a live and functioning organism. In short, I can't sleep,
I live in constant pain, and I know that will imprison me in
this weariness of life (*taedium vitae*, as Horace called it) for
quite a few weeks to come. I know this from experience, and
also because I was attached several times to outpatient clinics,
particularly at the Sacré-Coeur Hospital in Cartierville, first as
a medical student and then as a doctor. But you know all this
already because I mentioned it before. So I will pass on to other
things, moving down one landing and taking up my position
so as to see what is coming on the page, before the very eyes
of the reader conditioned to this spectacle. I mean, in fact, the
incredible, the ineffable events that took place in Chivasso in
the night of August 9, 1536. Renata arrived very late that night
on the outskirts of the village of Chivasso. During the evening
hours following the dinner which the printer, Zimara, shared
with the writer, J. C. Beausang, Jules-César described, in his
intimate journal, the first symptoms of the typhoid fever he had
caught north of the Alps, somewhere in Neuchâtel or Martigny
or Brig (the typhoid epidemic took 987 victims in Brig in 1536,
1352 victims in Padua and more than 2000 in Venice that same
year). In those days they said "pandemic" to indicate this frightful
scourge, which Jules-César Beausang was one of the first to
see as being connected to a newly-recognized phenomenon: that
of contagion. But he had no time to elaborate his theory, as
he succumbed prematurely in the room of a Chivasso inn. His
last hours are known to us through the diary he kept — courage-
ously, it must be said — while the first pains shot on crossed
paths along their implacable destined way, so well described
at a later date by Girolamo Frascatoro. Jules-César Beausang,
passing for ambassador, was aware for quite a while after the
first signs appeared that he was mortally ill. Initially, he thought
himself the victim, for the first time in his life, of an epileptic

seizure; then, nauseated, he pushed his table closer to the open window (for he was suffocating); and it was then, through the open window that looked out into the Chivasso street in which Carlo Zimara had his printing shop, that he saw a young girl (Renata, beyond a doubt) enter the printer's, exhausted, staggering, and then (an hour later) saw the same young girl leave the printer's, escorted by Carlo Zimara's wife. The two women made off with all haste toward the west end of the village (on the road to Turin), seemingly distraught and anguished as if some frightful thing had taken place in the printing shop just before. But Jules-César Beausang had grown very feeble since that moment, he had taken stock of his cyanosis of the lips, his blackened belly, his lower limbs (turned blue), and this had been enough to tell him what was happening to him. And he had been filled with a great despair. His life was ended, truly ended. And he could not understand this brusque arrival of death, the shattering suddenness of total blackness (in stunning contrast to the ovoid white of budding life). The events in the printing shop had nothing to do with his manuscript. There was no way that he could have guessed this fact, but I can tell you quite simply, for we now know these things with an almost uncanny precision.

To start with, Renata arrived after dusk at Carlo Zimara's printing shop. She appeared haggard and had only only one thought in her mind: to hand over her manuscript at last and receive the promised number of ducats: viz, two hundred. Then she would leave that very moment for the discreet and shadowed glade where she had spent the night alone. That was a way she knew, that sinuous little road that followed the course of the Sesia. She had only to go back to the north-east, or toward the distant Alps that formed a nyctalopic chain, an impassable wall by night. But when she arrived at the shop the printer — Carlo Zimara — had made quite a pleasant fuss over her, taking his time. He, of course, was determined to verify the authenticity of a manuscript that reached him by this route, and he suggested to the girl that she rest in a corner of his shop, a spot, in fact, which he must have used as his office, for there was a lamp there, and a desk, and a table, and a kind of couch where Renata stretched out at her ease and, after a few seconds vacillation, fell sound asleep. The printer, as soon as he saw the pretty smuggler was sleeping, left his manuscript and came near the girl, who was by now in a deep slumber. He stood admiring her. And, without waking her, he proceeded to subtract certain elements of her dress which made her seem even nearer and more attractive in his eyes. Her breast was now totally bared to the printer's gaze. He could not resist the urge to touch her there, timidly, with his fingertips. As this did not wake her and she remained in her deep trance, motionless and snoring, he proceeded with greater haste to undress her. He would take advantage of this chance partner's sleep to divest her of all her clothes without her knowledge; he would go on with impunity as she lay there on his couch (where he could give free rein to his initiative). When he had partially undressed her she emerged from her torpor and tried with every possible means to repulse this stranger (the printer); but too late. Carlo Zimara was beyond all reasoning and was well on his way to satisfying his lust. Stronger than she, he held his prey in his arms and arrived very soon at his orgasm, violating her thus in her very existence and in the secret of her maidenhood. Carlo Zimara grunted a few times, then collapsed, replete, on Renata Belmissieri who, for her part, horrified, had been conscious through it all. Zimara the printer, like a sated beast, out of breath and running with sweat, crashed awkwardly on top of the girl, horridly relaxed. He went to sleep in this position, while Renata again became prey to those hypersynchronic shocks whose terrifying mechanism was so familiar to her. She was well aware that a seizure was under way. Electric discharges rocked and lifted her body with increasing violence and frequency, and the crisis seemed to be approaching its apnoea . . . She saw clearly this indecent creature prostrate on her body, naked, sleeping, while she, shaken with violent spasms, fell to the floor gyrating, biting her tongue, taking her companion with her. There on the floor, lying beside the girl in her convulsions, the printer in a panic made fumbling efforts to dress her again. Hasty attempts, clumsy, inappropriate, ineffectual. Gestures of shame and fear: yes, Carlo Zimara was afraid of the unbridled force in this girl of whom he had just now had his pleasure. But fear is a poor guide. Carlo Zimara would have done better to be frightened and let it go at that. But no, he grew curious, almost a voyeur, and then was possessed by a curious activity, busying himself with caresses which he lavished with impunity on the poor child, racked by her violent seizure. He knelt before Renata (who was in the torture of comatogenic discharges), caressing her (she was still unconscious) under her skirt, masturbating her clitoris with a kind of morbid, hypocritical, odious fervour. Poor Renata (O, my sister, my sister from the past!) howled, not with pleasure but simply in the course of her regular, implacable, intolerable shocks. She howled so loudly that Carlo's wife (sound asleep) awoke and appeared in the shop in her nightshirt, thinking her husband was being attacked by bandits. What she saw struck her as horrifying and unbelievable. She saw her husband Carlo kneeling before a poor girl, caressing her underhandedly without the creature's knowledge. Who was she then, this stranger who had come in the middle of the night to Carlos's shop? A girl from Turin, a whore beyond a doubt, a bitch who did it for money . . . She crept closer. Then she saw Carlo's miserable attempts to seduce this poor thing who appeared to be possessed of the demon. Horrors! How could this be? She knew well that all men were pigs, more or less — that much she'd been told! But Carlo, her own husband, a man of apparent integrity and respectability — how could she believe that he was like all the others, capable of the most swinish behaviour, of taking advantage of a poor sick girl only half conscious (almost unconscious), and trying to have his pleasure of her. What a horror!!! Totally under the spell of the girl's naked body, he had not taken the precaution of covering himself. He remained there, himself partially undressed, caressing the girl's lower body as if his life depended on it. Antonella felt such revulsion at the behaviour of Carlo that she picked up a lead matrix and stealthily crept closer to her husband. With all her strength she struck a blow with the lead matrix. Blood spurted from Carlos hair, and he fell back, but Antonella went on striking at his skull. She was half-lying on Carlo's body the better to reach her target, once, twice, three times, four times, five times . . . (She remembered no more than these five times, to which she later confessed). Renata, suddenly delivered from her aggressor, came to herself and tried to button her dress and lace up her bodice. Antonella's blows had resounded dully against the printer's skull, and his face was now covered with blood. Antonella rose and took a few steps toward the girl, who was beginning to recover her spirits. Now Renata was frightened that the woman might attack her and deliver another series of mortal blows. But Antonella, dropping the matrix whose letters rolled on the floor like so many dice, helped Renata to her feet. Antonella was weeping softly and uncontrollably, and she said to Renata:

"You see, I'm ashamed of my rage, but I am a thousand times more ashamed to have been married to this man."

And Renata Belmissieri and her new friend Antonella Zimara fled, taking a few belongings and certain bundles of banknotes of which Antonella knew the hiding-place. They left by night and took the road to Turin. Jules-César Beausang, from his open window, saw them run west, in the direction of Turin . . .

The Antiphonary

He had no more than a few hours to live; and the poor doctor spent them recapitulating his childhood in Ghent, and his wanderings as a student to Leyden and on to Bois-le-Duc, to Antwerp, Utrecht, Breda (in its full effervescence of Calvinism), and Malines; then Wittenberg, Groningen, Magdeburg and Lübeck. He recalled these years as one long exaltation, a slow and intimate religious revolution that had transformed him, the young Beausang, into an impenitent Gomarist. But when he had returned to Ghent, what had been his surprise to find that Calvinism was everywhere triumphant. The Gomarists were supreme in Dortrecht and Amsterdam and to some extent in the larger cities of the United Provinces. But there was no climate of tolerance; and Jules-César Beausang, turned Gomarist in a world bubbling with change (Ghent), exiled himself to Basel where Oecolampadius had founded a reformed religion that was infinitely more open and humanist. He recalled, finally, his marriage to the younger sister of Guy de Brès in Saint Bavon's church in Ghent. But this marriage, which brought him three daughters, turned out disastrously. In his depression Jules-César Beausang had preferred to run like a coward from Ghent (and all his past) to exile in Basel on the shores of the Rhine, whose dense, dark stream continued, while he lived out his death-agony in a Chivasso inn, to roll majestically toward the North Sea. A few days later, beside the despairing lines of his journal, the body of the famous doctor was discovered, and thrown in the pauper's grave of Vercelli, a neighbouring town. This was the fate of all those struck down by the epidemic.

48

The Antiphonary

San Diego. We must not forget the good things of this world. The pharmacist — damned pervert — who smiled at me in San Diego as he held out a block of prescription forms and a pen, had a number of things in mind which were not in mine at that precise moment. I should have been more suspicious, but like an incurable fool I marched toward my misfortunes with no idea of what awaited me. When I think of it I have a vague desire to vomit — a powerful, irresistible nausea, and I reach out for an unattainable basin of sky-blue enamel in which I would like to puke out my soul. But I have only green bile which I spit out with difficulty and some spasmodic effort. Oh, poor me, poor Christine, poor Renata, poor Christine, poor Beausang dying in the room of a Chivasso inn, just up the street from the printing shop where Antonella is coldly (if one may say so) murdering her lust-maddened husband. Two days have not been enough to recover from the horror of San Diego, not only the horror of the Hillcrest Motel, but the still more frightful horror that resulted from my visit to the drugstore in the San Diego shopping centre. To be sure, I was bruised and abominably massacred, and lacked poise with the pharmacist. He saw that I was having some trouble (and for good reason: my wrist was hurting abominably) in writing the prescription I wanted him to make up for me (for me, a doctor passing through San Diego, a doctor atrociously disfigured, desperate, beaten, unable to write in a straight line the few words I needed to get this prescription going). Liquid Demerol in pills of 500 mg. But that was probably too strong for me. I was almost paralyzed, with a hemiplegic stroke, the fasciculi crossed — as in the illustrations of Jean-Etienne de Calcar, my master, male version of myself, my double double, and the only double to resemble me totally with his interlacing figures of the Vesalian anatomy, his Principle of Life, his mysteries, his unpredictable turns, his multiple, labyrinthine configurations. Yes, I am the only enduring and authentic (or inauthentic) copy of Jean-Etienne de Calcar, official creator of anatomical drawings for Andreas Vesalius! Yet what could be less authentic than this carbon copy I have become under the strong, pressurized and equal strokes of the San Diego pharmacist? He gave me something, a 293 pill or something of the sort, to help overcome my pain, poor beaten-up woman that I was, and he took me back to his dispensary, a cramped little room just big enough for two. There was a red couch, obviously very old, and an adjustable relaxing-chair. He showed me first to the chair, which reassured me a little. I lay down in it and at once felt the irresistible drowsiness caused (though I didn't know it then) by nothing else than the 293 pill. I quickly reached the profound conviction that he had given me something other than a 293. A kind of heaviness slid into my body, a general torpor. Suddenly my eyelids and my limbs were leaden. My legs were abnormally heavy. I felt like a statue hunched into an ill-fitting concrete cast — something of the sort. I know that I gave in to sleep without the slightest resistance. I must have been motionless and snoring loudly. Snoring, my legs spread wide — or in some such position. I don't know how long I remained thus hypnotized, under the effects of a so-called ''293'' that I had swallowed in good faith. Then, when I awoke, I discovered the pharmacist in my field of vision, kneeling, it seemed to me, just below my thighs and trying to undo my stocking-catches and (laboriously) free me of my stocking-belt and my underpants. I was not horrified, not even shocked. I was flooded by a kind of well-being that left me soft, feeble, incapable of moving, and above all unable to do anything to stop the unctuous approach of the pharmacist. And yet I saw him leaning over me, humped like a poor dog on a bitch, able to see no more than the turquoise-blue line of my panties (I may not have mentioned that he was short-sighted). I succeeded, miraculously, in articulating a few words such as, "What are you doing there?" or, "Please stop, I beg you . . . " But he smiled at me, and said aloud (as if he were speaking to someone else), "Yes, you know, when a pretty lady comes along and wants a little dope, why, we try to oblige . . . " I succeeded in getting out the following words (though ever so feebly): "But the Demerol wasn't for me . . . " (And I had a flash of Jean-William prostrate across the bed). Too late, too late, the druggist had not heard my plaintive voice, and he systematically continued his preliminary inspection. Once he had unhooked my stocking-belt and removed my panties edged with pink lace, I was, to all intents and purposes, at his mercy, naked, completely open to him, and almost an accomplice of what he was, with some difficulty (because of having kept his pants on) preparing to do, that is, enter into me, penetrate my body with his penis intact and hard as a hazel-tree branch in springtime, long as a Pacific peninsula, stiff as a judge! I was entranced like a Buddhist monk, hypnotized by this Trajan column of twisted braid, all covered with sculptures in relief (you see what I mean — a touch of drugs and you're off and dreaming). But it's true, my fascination numbed me strangely, and I let myself be won over by the slippery hardness of the pharmacist — by this foreign body which suddenly opened me completely and, without wounding me, entered my body like a gentle sword, like a medieval dagger (there are tons of medieval daggers in the Hague museum in the Netherlands); long it was, interminable, cutting, rapid and then, oh, very slow, poised within the tenderness the pharmacist gave to his caresses and the regular-

The Antiphonary

ity of his movements of retreat and re-entry. Oh, truly, you will never know — or rather it's I who will never know all that happened in the office of a druggist in San Diego while Jean-William was supposedly, simultaneously, at the Hillcrest, gasping on the floor in a half-wrecked room. I had come to this pharmacy to get liquid Demerol which I would subsequently have injected in Jean-William in order to soothe him. But, oh darkened heavens! this nameless pharmacist had infused me with dried snake-bite remedy or, more diabolical still, a hallucinogenic drug in capsule form, and I was off in seventh heaven, elated, filled with this modest little druggist whose steel blade, tungsten alloyed, transpierced me as Cupid's arrows pierced the ecstatic heart of Bernini's St. Teresa. I was irrigated by the tiny channels that form a divine network throughout my whole body. All gentleness had suddenly disappeared under the impulsion of this whole enterprise of rape and hallucination! It was a strange pleasure, that pleasure of mine: interlarded with remorse, filled with formal innovations, with the flux and reflux of blood turned wild in the genital transaction! Please do not think me irresponsible! I truly acted in good faith when the pharmacist proposed that I swallow on the spot that non-authentic capsule which resembled a ''293''. What is more, I had gone there with the sole purpose of finding a remedy likely to calm the uncontrolled spasms of Jean-William. Would you, dear reader, have thought that I was about to fall — at that moment in time — into an ambush? Did you think that in taking that nameless capsule I was swallowing a fatal philter that would prepare me for any folly? I was bruised from head to foot, covered with contusions and hematic discolourations, physically less than myself. It could not have entered my mind that in that state (and I mean my state when I set foot in the pharmacy) I was on the point, shall we say, of experiencing a grandiose and monstrous adventure such as this! I would never have thought that an ordinary man (normal, shall we say) could

feel the slightest desire for the poor ragbag I had become —
after the battle in the Hillcrest Motel. Still less did I fear this
kind of seduction. Could it be that I was seductive? No, I must
be hateful, ugly, distasteful, repugnant — like a woman emerging
alive from an auto accident that has claimed three instant dead!

But alas! I now have to get it through my head that what
happened was perfectly normal. Ugly and all, I was still desirable
to a man with an obsession, one who had spent the day taking
a series of drugs each more fascinating than the last. And he
desired me with an efficiency as rewarding to him as to me.
I was exalted by his frantic desire for the final pleasure, by
the approach of his convulsive peak, by the amorous tempest
that roiled his lower body and spread through him to all his
members, striking finally at my belly, my own poor belly, and
propagating its waves to the extremities of my body, and, by
reaction, waking me . . .

Waking was frightful. Not only did I see myself as having
been raped by this druggist who had so cleverly dosed me that
I had no resistance left, but I awoke, after falling into a profound
sleep (consecutive to my irresistible orgasm and perhaps to the
absorption of a soporific whose formula was unknown to me),
in the dispensary of the druggist all alone and naked. He had
left me in that incredible state, my cinnabar dress crumpled in
a heap on the floor, my underclothes scattered to the four winds
in this sordid little room. I had no notion of the passage of
time nor how late at night it was. I stood up in the middle
of the room. I saw a scrap of paper laid precisely on my crumpled
dress. I leaned down and read: "Dear love, your case is probably
desperate. When I saw you coming to me in that state I knew
you would do anything to get your regular dose of morphine.
So I gave it to you. Take my advice, don't get yourself into
that state in any dirty joint with (maybe) members of the Cosa
Nostra. If you wake up before I come back, please drink the

whole glass I prepared for you. It's right beside your bra. Don't hate me too much. I'll be back tomorrow morning at 8'clock sharp. But really, I thought last night that you were threatened in some way. That's why I had the idea of keeping you overnight. Bob.''

What a swine, I thought. What an unpardonable swine!!! I couldn't get over his version of what had happened, so convenient for his lust, the pig!!! But this was not a time for hanging around, for it was already 4 o'clock (in the middle of the night). I slipped quickly into my dress and reached for the phone. No, I thought — and ran to the front door of the brightly-lit store. Not a chance: it was locked, and, what was more, a silver strip parallel to the frame showed that there was a confounded alarm system. I went back to the telephone, a secretarial model with 4 or 5 lines. I quickly found a phone book for greater San Diego in which (as was only to be expected) the telephone number of the Hillcrest was listed. I wrote it on a note-pad near the phone. I hesitated for a long time before dialling the seven figures of this number, for I had no story ready for Jean-William to explain why . . . But what was there to explain? I had nothing to say to him. He had no right to an explanation from me after what had happened between us the evening before.

I was there, alone, in that deserted pharmacy, wandering among the brightly-lighted aisles. I saw myself pass in the great mirrors that lined the walls behind the shelves of medicaments and beauty aids. There were mirrors everywhere, and I collided constantly with my own image, not without feeling a well-founded horror at the sight of myself. I discovered a drawer that contained a variety of hemostatic pencils and painted my many contusions with one, softened under the office tap. Just look at her: it's poor Christine, it's me, painting away at her face like a boxer. And I talk about her in the third person (and surprise myself by doing so — I suppose with reason) because I am this poor

The Antiphonary

bitch, Christine, doctor to the poor, beaten and beaten again by her husband, raped on the run by an elegant druggist, humiliated in the most impossible way. That long night (in the pharmacy) was more of the same. I emptied drawer after drawer of cauterizing and astringent agents, and other drawers of cosmetics (which helped me to mask my blessed face as best I could).

That's how the time went by. I was a prisoner in this pharmacy, and cursed every minute of it. I had to wait for the druggist to come back at 8 o'clock to escape from my prison. Toward 7 o'clock I finally had the strength to dial the number of the Hillcrest and ask to speak with Mr. Jean-William Forestier. The motel answered and asked me to wait and I heard the ring for his room. Once, twice, three times, four, five, six, seven, eight times it rang. The reception desk of the Hillcrest interrupted on the line to tell me that no doubt Mr. Forestier, at this hour of the morning ... And I said firmly that that was impossible, this was a very important call etc. In short, they let it ring, I don't know how many times.

"Jean-William!" I repeated his name over and over when I heard the receiver lifted at the other end. But no one answered. No one even said hello. Could it be Jean-William who picked up the phone? Hard to say; impossible, in fact. I was at the other end of the line, left to my torment, speaking — but speaking to no one, on an open line that seemed nonetheless like a great gulf of darkness. I was stunned. I hung up without saying another word. I was thunderstruck, guilty and terrified at the same time. I had no idea what had happened to Jean-William during my escapade in this San Diego pharmacy. It was almost 7 thirty and I was stamping the floor with impatience. I wanted that druggist to arrive and deliver me once and for all from this dark detention (habeas corpus). The few touches I gave to my make-up kept me busy until 7 fifty-five — a few minutes before his return — and I then took up my post behind the counter to the right of the street door, that is, looking out on the shopping centre of San Diego (or was it South San Diego? I'm no longer sure).

The Antiphonary

My trip to Drummondville with Robert (Bernatchez) seems to me — from my personal perspective — a gust of joy and happiness that now, unavoidably, fills me with longing. We had registered at the Motel de l'Étoile on the shores of the Saint-François River, around 8 in the evening, after a political tour punctuated with speeches by Robert in each town we visited. Windsor, Richmond, Warwick, Acton Vale, L'Avenir, these names drift into my consciousness and intoxicate me still. The last meeting was to take place that very evening in Drummondville, at the Civic Centre. By 8 o'clock Robert and I were already exhausted, especially Robert, and we had just an hour to take a light supper and get to the Civic Centre where Robert had to make his entry at 9 without fail. I was lying on the bed, completely dressed, when Robert, emerging from a brief visit to the toilet, found me fast asleep. He was lying on top of me, and I could feel his breath, so close was his face to mine. I awoke in this position. Robert was smiling.

"You were sleeping?" he said.

"Yes."

"You are beautiful, Christine. And you don't want to get a divorce and marry me? Why? Would life with me be so dull? I'm trying to understand."

Well, I jolted myself as wide awake as I could to deal with this kind of question. And I realized that after all I could hardly give him a candid answer. How could I tell Robert — coldly — that I loved him but that a long time before I had married another (Jean-William) and, as a result, had given up my career as a woman doctor.

"Are you pained, Robert?" I asked him gently.

"You know very well it's on your account that I'm pained, as you call it. You married Jean-William Forestier, didn't you? And since you did, a long time ago, I've been like a fifth wheel in your life! Sure you'd like our love to go on, but in secret, as if it were just an affair."

"No Robert, don't say that!"

"It's the truth," he said coldly. "You don't talk to me the way you used to. Jean-William's name is taboo between us, you never tell me what you do when I'm not with you. You're putting off our meetings more and more. Before, we were always together. Now that's changed. You like me well enough, but you want me not to make any demands, just be at your beck and call and mostly not around — because after all it's safer not to play with fire."

I didn't know what to say.

"Don't worry. I won't force you to talk to me; never fear."

Robert got up and went away from me, leaving me alone and disconcerted on the bed. He had no heart for anything, not for our love, not even for the speech he was making that evening. He had the text in his hand. Mechanically he laid the few typed sheets on the dresser, went and shaved, changed his shirt, re-tied his tie, and all without a single glance in my direction. It was as if I had suddenly disappeared or been swallowed by an abyss. I had no more weight, no more interest, not even the semblance of female seductiveness in Robert's eyes. He had just condemned me to the most intolerable kind of non-existence. I was nothing, nothing, a poor desolate girl, worthless, inadequate to the demands of life, and — above all capable of lying to the man she loved, the man who loved her.

"Where are you going?" Robert asked, as I got up from the

bed and started towards the bath.

"I'm ... going to have a shower. Do I have enough time?"
He consulted his wrist-watch and nodded.

I showered quickly and came out without drying, naked, dripping with water and bath foam, with only the bath-towel for a robe (can you call it a robe?). I rubbed my legs, leaning against the edge of the bed. Robert was there. I felt him very close to me physically, drawn by my exhibition, caught despite himself by a sudden desire — at this instant, in the motel — and capable of taking me violently just before leaving for the meeting. I must admit that I had, with some measure of coquetry, wished for exactly that. And now Robert, disconsolate, was looking at me sadly and without desire. His sadness won out over any other feeling; and I, within touching distance, no longer inspired in him as in the past that rush of feeling, that vital current, the desire I had so often been able to provoke in him. His sadness submerged me, somehow, in a dark, dull stream. I was no longer the woman he loved, but a vulgar creature trying to force his desire without being able to provoke it effectively. Oddly enough, his resistance shocked me. I felt a kind of aggressive irritation against it. And in a few seconds I had turned quite against him, become his enemy and not his love. Poor me, poor Robert ...

Robert, confirmed in his attitudes, dared to defy me. He was humiliating me outright (though of course I didn't realize all this at the time: I was too busy *feeling* humiliated to be conscious it was happening) but I think now that he knew his attitude was vindictive, intensely vindictive, consciously vindictive. I knew that he was hurting me in my most sensitive point. Yes, and what was more, he was revealing that vulnerable point to me. I had never known the extent to which I was physically dependent on the pleasure I experienced with a partner. This was a dark and shameful revelation to me; but I don't think Robert noticed that. Or perhaps he understood it perfectly, perhaps he had arranged the whole thing, set the scene against me knowing exactly what he was doing. (If I had him in front of me now I'd blacken his face with bruises, I'd pound his whole body.)

Not because he exposed my vulnerable point to me but because he made me talk afterwards, made me talk and talk and tell him (in tears) all my troubles and the truth, the hateful truth. I confessed to everything I had experienced before I met him and even the most remote incidents of my childhood — the most embarrassing as well: the ones involving my father (the business of attempted rape), my initiation into debauchery (with student acquaintances), and all the ramifications of the triangle formed by Jean-William, himself (Robert) and me. In this connection he was satisfied by nothing less than the whole story: the time of every rendezvous, details of every encounter with Jean-William and with him (Robert), my sequence of physical pleasure at every meeting, down almost to the timing of my orgasms, the index of intensity of my post-coital collapse, the coefficient of my hyposalivation and of my vaginal emissions, the quantity of sperm of each man, the contraceptive methods used in each case, the words spoken before and after each time, every word, every intonation, every scrap of emotion, every little gasp or sigh or gesture — however indecent the description might become — every tiniest gesture in the venereal process of each encounter — my God, it was frightful!!! I was in tears, but Robert told me coldly to get on with my abominable confession. He interrogated me with a cool rage (typical of him), holding a glass of scotch in his right hand. It had very little water and several ice-cubes. Oh! I begged for pity, I prayed him to stop this unbearable interrogation. Robert refused and announced without the slightest emotion that he was quite willing to forego his meal in order to continue this ''conversation'' up to the last moment before leaving for the Civic Centre.

I don't know if Robert, a follower of the theories of the Aquinate, considers *claritas* as integral to amorous relationships, or if he favours *resplendentia*. All I know is, he would have killed me that night to find out everything, to elucidate and understand everything! My *resplendentia* was nil, but there was a mad *claritas* that triumphed in this perverse conversation which concentrated in fact only on details that were sure to humiliate me.

Let things once get out of balance and everything goes haywire! I know that to my sorrow. As Beauduin of Canterbury said, *"Parilitas autem dimensionis secundum aequalitatem, simili-tudinem, compositionem et commensuratam . . . . Quod debitam mensuram minuit vel excedit, vel ad sui comparis similitudinem non accedit, gratia pulchritudinis non vetustat."* A succulent text, full of a profound obsession with the deforming malignity that can strike a woman . . . or a couple (but this Beauduin of Canterbury does not make explicit!). Translucid (before Robert's cruel eyes) I disintegrated into a haphazard collection of particles of ugliness and small stains which, in their insensate orbits, recom-posed my already distorted image — in negative and enlarged.

Only time could have saved me; but Robert made me speed up the parade of other men who touched me, possessed me, loved me . . . Caught in this game, I know no woman who would not have been dizzied and carried away by vanity. And I, poor fool, gave in like that. Dizzied and vain, I was, as it were, invaded by this whole succession of amorous (or venereal) partners whom Robert forced me to describe in detail. I think he might even have given up his political meeting at the Drummondville Civic Centre if I had stretched out the list of my encounters. But this was not the case, for well before 9 o'clock I had finished the whole thing. Giving in to his interro-gation I went faster and faster, and always with fewer scruples (or less guilt) and succeeded in giving him everything he expected from this confession. Robert had had time (as I went on with my shameful self-exposure) to pour a second glass of Chivas

Regal. I was veiled (ever so slightly) by the large towel I had wrapped around me, and prostrate on the bed. I was at the end of my strength and couldn't understand what Robert wanted to achieve with all this. Long silences occurred between us. He no longer answered my questions, and seemed in no way touched by my tears. He sipped away at his Chivas Regal and with the other hand held the typewritten pages of his speech.

"And your profession," he said. "Why did you give up medicine? Your practice, I mean?"

"I've told you a thousand times: because of Jean-William!" (I was beside myself, exasperated by my own self-criticism.)

"Ah!!!" he said, thinking that one over.

He calmly took a mouthful of scotch and went on: "Do I understand you to say that Jean-William insisted on your giving up your profession of medicine?"

"No!!!" I cried, impulsively, "of course not!"

There was silence again. I couldn't open my mouth, but I knew that for some reason he was simmering. He knew something, or had guessed something.

"Do I have to ..." (I stopped, for no good reason, but I was in a panic, and shaken by his quiet assurance). "Oh, what does it matter? You might as well know. I got pregnant last year, by accident, and ... I had an abortion. By an accommodating colleague."

"Who was it?"

"That made me pregnant?"

"Yes, who?"

"An American professor — of medicine — I met him at the home of friends."

"You mean he didn't even leave a visiting card?"

"Do you want to know his name? Is that it? Robert W. Shact, a graduate in cardiology from John Hopkins."

"Did you see him again?"

The Antiphonary

"Yes, I suppose so. But not often, for he was here only six weeks, at the Institute of Cardiology."

"Did he know he'd made you pregnant?"

" . . . Yes. And now what? How many times did I see him? Where did I see him, and what else?"

"You say this happened last year. When, exactly?"

"February or March, I think. Robert, don't make my cry like this. I can't take any more. I'm ashamed of myself and you seem to be trying to make me more ashamed!"

But Robert didn't listen to my groan of protest. He drank his scotch quietly and looked at his watch (8:40).

"February or March last year. But we were in love then, you and I, and we'd said we were in love. I still don't understand why you gave up medicine. I don't see the connection."

I was finished, my will-power was turned to mush, I was completely feeble. I suddenly saw myself through the eyes of the man I loved, the man I had loved, who still loved me. I was ugly, and couldn't stand myself. And so I wept all the tears I had left, my head burrowed in the pillows.

"I asked you a question," said Robert calmly.

"Yes . . . I know . . . The connection. It's this." (I would tell the whole story, whatever the consequences.) "The other doctor . . ."

"The accommodating colleague?"

"The other doctor had agreed to do the abortion because he wanted to sleep with me. He refused the money we had agreed on. And he asked me to come back to his private clinic a few weeks later, just to see if everything was in order. That's when I understood. He only wanted to get me there, and he thought he had a hold on me through some kind of deontological obligation. But if there's anyone that revolts me physically, it's him. I couldn't stand the man . . . At this point he started getting very clever, and went so far as to blackmail me about the abortion.

The Antiphonary

I was scandalized and furious. I threatened to report him to the College of Physicians, but he had seen that one coming. He proved that I could do nothing to him for the good reason that the private clinic (where he had aborted my baby) was in fact an office he had never rented personally, but had borrowed from a colleague. And he even had an alibi. During the operation patients had been waiting for him in his real office. I was paralyzed. His real office! I could never have believed it would end that way. I left that old maniac's office like a storm. I never set foot in it again, believe me!"

"I do," said Robert. "I believe you. Damn, it's ten to nine. My meeting ... "

All he did was get up, go out of the motel and leave me alone and weeping on the bed, ruined, humiliated at having told the story of my life, really (or so I told myself) on the verge of a nervous collapse. And he, hard and implacable, he went away intact. His image, too, was untouched. Today, still, when I think of him, I see him as the perfect man, worthy, impeccable, strong and very independent. I know that he married Suzanne Polack, very pretty, very rich, but unable, I'm sure, to make him happy or satisfy him. And my one achievement was to make him miserable. What a pitiful triumph!

The Antiphonary

"Woman's beauty is the symbol of all the beauty in the universe," wrote Duns Scotus. *"Mulier est sensus corporeus,"* he continues, *"naturaliter humanae naturae insitus, per quam, in hic videlicet qui perfecti sunt, visibilis creaturae pulchritudo ad laudem Creatoris refertur ..."* I don't know if I feel an exaggerated delight in this passage — by one of the "total Averrhoists," as we like to call Duns Scotus, Cassiodorus, Boetius, Abbon of St. Germain, Osborn of Gloucester, Hraban Maur and the celebrated Rémi d'Auxerre. All these thinkers — and many others — are well-known to me, for in the course of doing research for my thesis it occured to me that I should skim through those writers who were, for a Jules-César Beausang or a Pompanazi, the great "modern" philosophers — the "ancients" being Aristotle, Plato, Plotinus, Heraclitus and Zeno of Elca. It happened that I took pleasure in reading these so-called "modern" writers, allowing my *delectio* to take precedence — as was predictable — over my *fruitio*. God knows my delectation was long and beneficial, like the enjoyment experienced by a Jules-César Beausang, who at several points in his works includes long quotations from great writers such as Honorius of Autun, Williram of Ebenberg, Duns Scotus, Saint Bonaventure, Orderic Vital, Rupert of Deutz, not to mention Guillaume d'Auvergne and the Aquinate, all of whom had a particular influence on him. And I have forgotten to mention such important names as Gérard d'Abbeville, Alexandre de Halles and the well-known Adam of Belladonna.

But why bother listing them all? The more so as this is almost an impossible task. The plethora of theory in the middle ages can well be described as inexhaustible. Its richness is diffusive, the movement of its thought anaclastic; why, then, try to isolate and describe it as if we were dealing with a thin, wavering line? Nothing captures the spirit of the age better than the metaphor of light, whose property it is to distribute itself, to propagate itself, to radiate and bring warmth.

The *Theatrum Chemicum,* published towards the beginning of the Renaissance (though anonymously), had an astonishing success — in precisely the style of those diffusive, expansive Middle Ages. On that August 10 of 1536, in Turin, the abbot Leonico Chigi was reading the *Theatrum Chemicum* as he paced up and down in the little garden that was the inner courtyard of the San Tomaso parish presbytery. At least so goes his minute description of how he passed his time on that memorable day. And suddenly two women, heavily veiled, burst into the presbytery garden. Abbot Chigi, putting his book aside, recognized the wife of the printer Zimara running toward him. She was breathing heavily (so he wrote that very evening in his notebook). She informed him, in the presence of another woman (not known to the priest) that her husband Carlo had just been murdered. This was a shock to Chigi, who was a long-standing friend of the printer of Chivasso.

"We must call the police," he said. "Was it bandits? Would you recognize them?"

But Antonella caught his arm and begged him to speak softly.

"No," she said to the young priest, "it was not bandits. I killed him."

Leonico Chigi later described this scene, and admitted that he fainted when Antonella revealed to him the crime against Zimara.

When he regained consciousness he was in the presbytery, with Antonella and the unknown woman by his side. They had brought him to his own bed. And suddenly (just remembering) he thought he knew who the other woman was, or rather, the girl, for she had come to him a few weeks before and he had directed her then to Carlo Zimara in Chivasso, or rather to San Bernardino, near the border. He also recalled how she had confided in him the matter of her strange illness (the falling sickness), and how moved the young Turin priest had been by her story. But what was her name? He couldn't remember. Had she even told him her name?

Collecting his wits, Leonico Chigi stared at Renata and said:

"My child, I have already seen you somewhere. I am certain of it. Tell me, are you a messenger of the Pope, or ..."

"My name is Renata Belmissieri, and I did come to see you a while ago. And after we had spoken you let me sleep in your bed until sunrise."

Thus the scene continued among the three protagonists. The abbot Chigi finally remembered where and how he had seen Renata, and Antonella recounted in detail the incident of the death of Zimara the printer. It was then that she gave him the precious manuscript of Jules-César Beausang, whose *Treatise* and *Commentaries on Aristotle's Physics* the abbot Chigi had already read. He was thus in a position to know what a priceless manuscript he had before him.

When he had recovered from his first emotion he invited Antonella to confess in due form — to himself, of course — and asked Renata Belmissieri if she would wait until Antonella was finished before making her own confession. It was thus agreed that Renata should wait in the church of San Tomaso, close by the confessional of the abbot Leonico Chigi. And this was done.

When Renata's turn came she entered the narrow, austere confession box, but already the warning signs of her seizure were upon her. She was in a sweat and stammering, and afflicted with passing states of confusion (or profound troubles of the mind). Abbot Chigi feared the worst. As there was no one in the church he decided to transport Renata into the sacristy. Antonella, who was waiting nearby, helped him to carry poor Renata at arm's length. Abbot Chigi and Antonella succeeded in laying her out in the main room of the sacristy in the midst of the vestments and holy sacraments which were lying there higgledy-piggledy. Antonella withdrew at a sign from the young priest. And he stayed alone with the sick girl, who was now prey to the hypersynchronic shocks of the disease. He called upon the Holy Ghost, the All-Powerful God of the Diseased; but this was of no help, and poor Renata Belmissieri was abandoned to the increasingly violent spasms of her attack ...

The Antiphonary

"If thou knowest not, O fairest among women," says the Bridegroom (in the Song of Songs), "Rise up, my love, my fair
one, and come away ... Behold, thou art fair, my love, behold
thou art fair; thou hast dove's eyes within thy locks; thy
hair is as a flock of goats ... Thy teeth ... thy breasts ...
thy temples ... thy neck ..."

Leonico Chigi's voice had grown emphatic as he read this
passage to Renata, who was beginning to recover from her fit.
She was stretched out on an altar in the sacristy of the church
of San Tomaso, while her friend Antonella kept watch outside
the sacristy door. The abbot Chigi, kneeling near Renata, continued his reading of the Song of Songs, alternating it with the
Commentary of Origen which is built around the allegories
implicit in the holy text. And Chigi translated freely from this
Father of the Church: "This means not to descend within thyself
and go back to the causes of thy being, but rather, to contemplate
thy beauty and trace back to its causes." And the abbot began
quoting Origen in Latin: *"Nisi cognoveris temetipsan, o pulchra
inter mulieres — i.e.: o anima, et agnoveris et pulchritudinis
tuae causas ince descendere, quod imaginem Dei facta es ..."*

And as Origen obviously wants to conclude: "Beauty perceived
is a revelation of a higher beauty; and in the materialization
of the latter resides a special aesthetic value." All these enigmatic
arabesques in the thought of Origen enwrapped Renata in a soft,
inescapable net. The texts of Origen (his commentaries on the
Song of Songs) had been translated into Latin by Rufino, and

69

it was this translation that the abbot held in his hand as he spoke to poor Renata, who was deeply moved by the very terminology of the Canticle. Never in her life had she heard such a touching sermon, with such beautiful words and such astonishing praise of love and beauty. She awoke to hear the trembling voice of the abbot Chigi reciting to her the most splendid passages in the Bible. Tears were in her eyes. She did not know how to suppress the sobs of passion and emotion that racked her, while the young abbot, concentrating on the sacred script, failed to notice his listener melting in tears and marvelling with such fervour at the majesty of the text. "Contemplate thy beauty and trace back to its causes ..." How that moved Renata and how beautiful it was, with an unspeakable, superhuman beauty ...

Renata, coming out of her comitial trance, entered an incommensurable mystical trance. She drifted with the voice of the young Turin priest and, at the end of her optical field, saw the naked body of the bride, and close by (equally naked) that of the bridegroom who, by chance, in this particular case, took on the appearance of the abbot Chigi. Naked, kneeling beside Renata, he was haloed with a marvellous beauty. Never in all her life had she seen such a beautiful man, nor one as inspired as this "bridegroom" (the abbot Chigi). But her vision, in its surpassing beauty, could not go on without unfolding a whole flora, secret and hallucinogenic, a forest, no less, of loving couples embracing and interlaced, naked, marvellously naked. And Renata and the abbot Chigi (her "bridegroom") were a part of the luxuriant vegetation of this mysterious forest. All this was so real that certain new physical sensations made themselves felt in Renata, in her very womb. And when the young priest (he too in the transports of an ill-ordered mystical state) touched her naked arm with his hand, Renata almost fainted, so strong was her emotion, close to the beginnings of a pleasure with whose unfolding delights she was completely unfamiliar ...

The Antiphonary

The abbot Chigi, aware of his erratic gesture, was himself deeply moved; but, more conscious than Renata, he wanted to go on to the end, whatever it might be, of this new discovery: the physical love of a woman.

Renata Belmissieri played the part of the Bride in the Song of Songs: "Thou art fair, my love, thou art fair, thine eyes are pillars behind thy veil, thy hair is as a flock of goats, thy teeth ... thy breasts ... thy breasts ... Arise, my love, my fair one, and come ..." Renata allowed herself to be lulled by the psalmodic music of the Song of Songs. She was in ecstasy, she wanted to be the "fairest among women." She permitted the divine caresses of her mystical bridegroom. Her passivity could only favour the slow and tender gestures of the young priest. He continued to enfold her in a marvellous network of touches and caresses and kisses. She was so carried away by all this that she was not even conscious of her contortions when Leonico Chigi's kisses grew more urgent. But they had caught fire so passionately that both had lost their sense of reality and Renata found herself on the floor, back on a level with her lover, letting him undress her while she learned a new and sweet way to caress him beneath his cassock. Life was a kind of progressive ecstasy, spasmodic, like pain. Renata was not conscious of being, herself, more audacious than her discreet companion. In a kind of fury she began to strip his clothing from him, while he, with a full erection, tried madly to hold her so that he could enter her belly. But Chigi's caresses were so exciting and maddening that she began to feel strange rhythmic spasms in her lower belly, while the abbot groaned like a wild man and emitted a rich, white liquid that spurted from him with utter spontaneity! He had fallen forward on top of Renata, exhausted, emptied, almost unconscious. Renata, for her part, was out of breath, caught in the disorder of her opened skirts, covered with sperm, astonished, weeping like a poor creature who has just discovered

71

a mystery the world had taken pains to hide from her. She continued to breathe hard as if, possessed, she were obeying her unleashed demon, or as if she had climbed indecently on the back of some animal humped in interminable pleasure. She could not imagine — we may suppose — that the most violent copulation contained such limitless aphrodisiac properties.

A little sobered (but exhausted as well), the abbot Chigi had risen to his feet, buttoning his cassock. He was in a great sweat, his hair standing on end, his face haggard and guilty. But Renata Belmissieri was still contorting herself at his feet, emitting small, meaningless cries and raucous rattles, as if her amorous appetite was not in the least appeased.

Abbot Chigi moved a few steps away. He went to a basin of fresh water and splashed his face and hands. He looked at himself in the tiny glass that hung above the basin. Love — an astonishing and disturbing experience!

He heard steps approaching the sacristy. He was worried, but poor Renata seemed still to be dealing with her imprisoned demon. She lay on the floor, stretched out, partly undressed. Is it possible, the abbot Chigi asked himself, that she feels her pleasure with such intensity? The door opened suddenly. It was Antonella, all out of breath. She looked at Renata writhing on the floor and then at Chigi who was moving toward her, concerned. Antonella was glacial:

"The police are coming — to get her. What! That shocks you? Because you've taken a fancy to her little whore's body?"

"But what's come over you, my daughter? I do not understand. You mean that you have denounced this child?"

"I accused her of murdering Carlo, my husband. And if you don't testify to the same thing before the police I will denounce you as her accomplice. Here they come. Make up your mind. I leave you one chance."

"This is a horrible thing you have done."

The Antiphonary

"Never mind the morals, poor Leonico, and say the same thing I do or you're a dead man."

He had already agreed in his own mind. As the hob-nailed boots of the gendarmes resounded in the church of St. Tomaso the abbot Chigi lived through a nightmare. He looked down with tenderness at poor Renata (of whom he had taken such shameless advantage) and finished buttoning his soutane — following the suggestion of Antonella, whom he now began to detest.

As the gendarmes of Turin pushed into the sacristy they crossed themselves before the priest. Four of them took up their positions in the four corners of the room. Then, the sergeant made his entry.

"Good day, your Reverence." He looked down at Renata. "Oh, these girls! They're nothing but trouble. I hope she hasn't been too much bother to you, your Reverence."

"Not at all," replied the abbot.

"Well, let's have the facts, just as things happened." He took a notebook from his pocket. "Abbot ...?"

"Leonico Chigi is my name."

"C-h-i-g-i," the sergeant repeated slowly. "Now, you were in the confessional taking this girl's confession, and then ...?"

"Well, yes, yes I was," said Chigi, "I was taking her confession. But you must understand, the secret of the confessional prevents me ..."

"Oh, I understand," said the sergeant. "But I imagine you can describe to me what happened afterwards."

"All this is so distasteful," said Antonella. "I understand how the abbot feels."

"Well, you see, sergeant, when she began to scream I tried to get her to be silent, but she went on screaming and troubling people praying in the church. I knew that I could never control her with words, and so I came out and tried to bring her here by force, and ..."

"It was then," said Antonella, "that his Reverence called on me, in fact, asked me to call the police."

"Yes," said abbot Chigi, "that was it. I asked this parishioner, whom I know well, to notify the authorities, for this young girl ... kept repeating that she had killed Mr Zimara and that that was only a beginning. She said loudly that she intended killing others in the same way she had killed Zimara. And I did not yet know (for the widow Zimara was waiting for me at the confessional) that this innocent young girl had in fact just come from Chivasso where she had committed the said crime on the person of the said printer Zimara. I thought at first she was raving, in some kind of mad fit."

"Of course," said Antonella darkly, "she told the truth and she is mad into the bargain. But she is a criminal! She robbed me of my husband, poor Carlo!" — and Antonella became the mourning widow.

"Poor lady," said the sergeant of the Turin police, with feeling, "what a sad day for you! I think we can get on with our work without troubling you further." And the sergeant pointed at Renata and nodded to his men. Two of them took her under the arms and the other two marched behind in case she should try to escape. Before leaving, the sergeant turned respectfully to the abbot:

"Your Reverence," he said pompously, "human justice will do the rest. I thank you for making my task the easier by telling us what you revealed just now. I think the girl will hang. Good day to you."

Antonella was standing close beside the abbot Chigi as the troop of Turin police took away Renata Belmissieri, unconscious, from the presbytery, to bring her to the women's prison situated just outside the city, near Superga.

There was a gaping silence between Antonella and the young

priest. She took a few steps, her head lowered as if in shame, around the abbot Chigi.

"You know," she said to him, "I had my reasons for making up that story of murder and accusing Renata. It's true, I acted badly, but I did it for love. Yes, I can say it. For love."

"I don't understand . . ." said the abbot Chigi.

She hesitated, pretending shyness, and seemed embarrassed at her avowal, exuding modesty.

"I know," she went on, "that I am unworthy of a man like you."

"But just now, before the police came, you were very different with me! You threatened me because I had sinned and I am a priest. And now you talk of love!"

(Privately, Leonico Chigi was more excited by Antonella's declaration than he cared to show. He recalled a passage in *DE AMORE LIBRI. "Amor est passio quaedam innata, procedens ex visione et immoderata cogitatione formae alterius sexus."* All these texts, filled with the most fervent praise of physical beauty, enflamed his imagination now that, seeing himself as an irredeemable sinner, he secretly cherished the idea of expiating in profane fire that other burning — profane but how ecstatic! — that he had felt with Renata. Antonella did not, to be sure, have the virginal beauty or the sweet, almost angelic look of Renata. But she knew the world. A widow, she must have known physical love. And there she stood before him, like the prefiguration of his fate. "The beauty of woman," he had read somewhere, "is like the colour of the flower. As the flower is withered by frost or destroyed by rime, woman is diminished by sickness or destroyed by time as it passes." But in the eyes of Chigi, Antonella possessed the ephemeral grace described by the anonymous poet whose line had just passed through his mind — or was it by Hugh of Saint Victor? Yes, Antonella had a powerful carnal suavity, the passing physical harmony — but all things pass — whose attraction he had secretly decided no longer to resist! *"O caritas quanta est victoria tua!"*

Antonella had a notion of all this. At least, she hoped for it. And, in fact, just as she wished, the abbot suggested at once that she flee with him forever! And he added that the manuscript of the celebrated doctor Beausang would bring them a handsome return if they knew how to negotiate it.

Antonella threw her arms around his neck to kiss him, but he pushed her coldly away.

"This is not the time."

"You are right."

"But come with me. Come up to my room and we can make our plans in peace."

"And you forgive me for what I did? About Renata?"

He paused for a while, then:

"Yes," he said to Antonella. "I forgive you. *Errare humanum est.*"

And they went off together, taking a secret passage that led them to the nuptial chamber.)

The Antiphonary

While Renata Belmissieri is being carried off to the women's prison near Superga, and Antonella (the wretched cheat) is intoxicating the abbot Leonico Chigi, and these two (new) lovers are preparing in the utmost secrecy their departure from Turin, I, Christine Forestier, am here, near San Diego, not in a suburb of Turin but in another one, a superb one, of San Diego, just to the north on the Pacific coast in San Modesto, at the Holiday Inn motel, room 224 (second floor), with air conditioning, a portable TV set, a view (when one wants to take the trouble to open the sliding curtains) of the gentle smog (a local product) of San Diego bay and also of the cliffs and escarpments which, in this region, prevent the sea from overflowing. In fact, I will not be staying long here. Two days have already passed since Jean-William's ninth fit, and I am still horribly beaten up and unable even to let the chamber-maid see me (to the point, believe it or not, where I order my meals from Room Service and hide in the bathroom when they arrive, leaving a tip for the waitress on the dresser under the pretext that I'm taking my bath). This is no way to live. I hurt all over, in every place where it's physically possible to hurt, after taking a super-going-over from my adorable husband, student of Arab customs. It's an utter drag.

To get out of the drugstore that morning I actually used my head to such advantage that I was surprised by my own ingenuity. I rammed the pharmacist, head down, and sent him flying. He crumpled up against a shelf of cosmetics, while I took advantage of his surprise (and his fall) to make my escape. Once outside, I ran as far as I could. Then I spotted a phone booth and ducked inside. I took my last dime, slipped it into the slot designed for the purpose and dialed the Hillcrest (a number I will know by heart for the rest of my days). I asked for the room of Jean-William Forestier. His voice sounded in my ear immediately, giving me the uncomfortable feeling that I was beside him again.

"Hello," he said.

"It's me," I said, "Christine. I called a while ago and someone picked up the phone but nobody answered. I didn't know what . . ."

"What did you want to tell me?"

His self-control disconcerted me completely. I was mystified by his ability to land on his feet, and by his self-assurance.

"What I wanted to ask you? . . . Why, Jean-William, I wanted to know if you were feeling better."

"Is that all?"

"Of course not. I wanted to know how you were, because of what happened. You know what I mean?"

"Yes, I see," said Jean-William. "Tell me, just exactly where did you phone from the first time?"

"I was just in a shopping centre, in San Diego."

"Oh. You weren't by chance in a pharmacy, the San Diego Drugstore?"

"But . . . how did you know?" (I was dumbfounded.)

"Yes or no?"

"Well, yes, as a matter of fact I was, but I must tell you how it happened. I went into that drugstore at about 11 last night, just before closing. And then after . . . don't you see? I was looking for some medication to dress my wounds. And when I asked . . . for the things I needed . . . well . . ." (my quick breathing betrayed me) " . . . I was drawn into a trap, with no idea of what . . . And then I was a prisoner inside that drugstore until dawn ..."

"Don't you find your story a little strange? Really, Christine, what do you take me for? Since when do people get caught in drugstores and stay locked in until sunrise??? Did you catch your dress in a self-locking cash register and couldn't get away? Or did you sprain your ankle? Was that it? Come on, you might as well admit it. You slept with the druggist on duty. And don't deny it, Christine."

"Very well, if that's what you want to know, if that's what you wanted to happen, set your mind at ease. My answer is yes ... Are you satisfied now? Yes, I made love with the druggist and it's because of him that I had to spend the night in that store, locked in and unable to get away."

Jean-William's voice was abnormally calm.

"Do you have any idea of his name, this druggist's name?"

"L. J. Gordon, I read it on the diploma framed behind the counter, along with all his permits, municipal, state, federal ..."

"Gordon."

"But, listen, Jean-William, how did you know I was in that drugstore when I phoned the first time? How?"

"Very simple. I immediately asked the reception clerk where my anonymous call was coming from. He found out, gave me the number, and when I came back to the room you were still on the line. I understood then."

"But, since when do you spy on me like this? That's detestable! Anyone would think you suspect me ..."

"Yes, perhaps. Let's say, for the last year and a half. I don't know exactly. Around the time when you began seeing Robert again. I know it was only a few times. Robert Bernatchez. You see what I mean?"

"But that means you don't feel any love for me, not truly, it means you've always treated me with suspicion, with a kind of mental reservation about my infidelity. It's hard to believe!

79

The Antiphonary

My God,'' I said, ''can it be possible?''

''Yes, my poor Christine, it is possible. That, in fact, is how things have been.'' And he hung up.

I was disconcerted. I stopped crying and wiped my eyes. And I started back toward the shopping centre where I had left the Cutlass (coloured burnt sienna) the day before, just in front of the drugstore. I walked quickly so that passers-by would not get a good look at me, for my black-and-blue face was worth a second look. When I saw the shopping-centre I was outside the central parking-lot and quite far from the Cutlass. I could see it pretty well. It was hidden from the pharmacy by another row of cars. Farther along, at the end, was the front of the pharmacy. Suddenly, what was my surprise to see Jean-William walking along in front of the shopping-centre windows, stopping in front of the drugstore!!! He hesitated, looked around, and went swiftly inside. My first fear was that he might see the Cutlass parked nearby and make off with it, using his keys. But no, he didn't even see it. Quickly, he went into the drugstore. So I had two or three minutes to reach the car and get away from this place. Jean-William, I thought, is sure to have a good look at the druggist (jealous as he is), until he works up a good retroactive rage against me. I knew a little about that kind of situation.

I crossed the four-lane street, catching a traffic-light at the corner. And I hurried toward the burnt sienna Cutlass. It was before 9 o'clock. Busy people were on their way to work. This was my chance. It wouldn't be long now. The Cutlass was not locked. I had the starter key. I put it in the ignition and then, at that very moment, I was almost paralyzed by the terrifying shock of what I saw from my present vantage-point. Jean-William (whom I could see perfectly clearly) had taken a pistol from his jacket pocket and was brandishing it under the druggist's nose. The latter, thinking he was doing the right thing, opened the cash and made a show of putting all the money it contained on the counter. But Jean-William had not budged nor changed his position. A shiver of horror went through me. The druggist patiently went on offering all his money, and even added his personal wallet. He seemed frightened, and the last thing he wanted to do was fight this hold-up, or what he thought was one. So he did not put up the slightest resistance. That was obvious. Jean-William looked quickly over his shoulder, and a second later the druggist threw back his head, and dropped, with an expression of pain on his face. Jean-William didn't even take the money. He walked coolly to the front door. I had just been witness to the unorthodox murder of a stranger, the druggist who had inseminated me the night before with his ambrosia. Dead without knowing why. Or, worse still, dead after a blinding flash of comprehension that the man pointing a pistol at him had not come to steal his cash. Nothing could seem more horrible, *be* more horrible. Jean-William had killed with the coldness of a monster, and with shattering efficiency. I crouched in the car, hoping that he wouldn't see its shape, nor recognize the colour (burnt sienna) of the car rented in his name. In fact, to my immense relief, he went out (after killing the druggist and carefully holstering his pistol) from the pharmacy like a client who has just bought a bottle of aspirin. I saw him go back the way he had come, passing the same windows he had passed before committing his frightful and horrid crime. Slightly reassured, but still suffering from the shock of what I had seen (a *happening*, a very odd one), I put the Cutlass in gear and somehow managed to drive out of the parking lot without further trouble. I said to myself, he had a pistol. Since when? And why did he go so far as to kill the druggist? These troublesome questions flowed through my mind without bringing any answers. I was shaken, my hands were trembling, my blood pressure was certainly abnormally high. In short, I was in a state of panic and confusion.

The Antiphonary

The pistol, I thought as I drove through the traffic-crowded streets of San Diego, he could easily have bought this morning when the gun-shops opened (at 8:30). Or, he'd had it all the time in his black suitcase without my knowing. But this last hypothesis seemed to me unlikely. Alas, I was more and more certain, since his seizure of yesterday, that Jean-William was seriously going to pieces. His violence had broken out first in the hotel, where I had been the victim of a kind of aggressive madness. I know from my medical treatises that certain forms of epilepsy are attended by murderous or suicidal episodes. In both cases the deranged behaviour of the epileptic patient tends toward brutal destruction of life, whether his own or another's. These cases are rather rare. At least I know of no doctors in Montreal who have encountered this kind of epilepsy. I myself had never seen or studied one during my time as neurological intern. The improbabilities are, I imagine, correlative to the probabilities, and from this we can deduce that the improbability or likelihood of aggressive epileptic manifestations are both possible. I know that this kind of reasoning is prevalent in mathematics. Probability and improbability are assimilated to simple possibles. From that point on nothing is, strictly speaking, impossible. For example, by manoeuvering the Cutlass in the streets of San Diego, after the death of the pharmacist, I could, let us say, fatally injure a pedestrian who would be none other than my own husband: Jean-William. Or, for that matter, one of the druggist's children. But nothing of the kind took place. These were possibilities, and they remained such. And I, privileged spectator of a murder just committed, I succeeded in controlling myself sufficiently to drive quickly to our motel (the Hillcrest) and have a porter open the door of our room so that I could take a few things which I threw quickly into a valise. For I told myself that I had a ten-minute start on the murderer even if he took a taxi right after the crime. I was right. I left our room and tossed

the bag (and two dresses) in the trunk of the Cutlass. I took
the wheel again, more self-confident than ever, and made off
in great style for the northern outskirts of San Diego, along
the Presidio Freeway (highway 201, north) and left this super-
highway at the San Modesto exit, a little satellite town, very
pretty, situated north of the bay of San Diego. But this is far
from the end of my travels, for tomorrow morning I'm moving
farther north. I will leave the car at one of the Hertz offices
near an airport where I can fly to Montreal. In today's San Diego
Telegraph there was a reconstruction of the druggist's murder,
done by a journalist from obvious external clues or objective
indications (biography of the druggist — age, 41, colour of hair,
eyes, the scene of the crime at 9 o'clock in an empty drug store)
but the journalist did not understand that the difficulty of the
crime was (from a police point of view) that the criminal had
no police record, and, what was more, had not stolen the money
placed on the counter; and that it was the druggist himself who
must ideally lead to the murderer, precisely because the crime
seemed to have no motive. According to a certain train of logic,
the motive must be very real if it was so invisible. Thus, the
motive must be related to the private life of the druggist! And
to find out more about him it would likely not be enough to
question his wife or neighbours, it would be necessary for the
sole eyewitness of the crime — myself — to go to the municipal
police station in San Diego and describe what she had seen,
what she knew, what she could interpret or explain. But as I
sit here, believe it or not, I repeat to myself that I most decidedly
do not want to turn up at the police station, nor at the editorial
office of the San Diego Telegraph, for I'm afraid that Jean-William
will jump at the chance, immediately afterwards, to kill me without so much as a by-your-leave. Not to go is worthy of blame,
even punishable by law. But I take my decision with quiet assurance and with no feeling of guilt. After all, I know very well

that I am not an accomplice in Jean-William's murderous act. Moreover, I have a certain horror of the dead druggist. His brutal death upset me because I witnessed it, against my will; but on the other hand I can only rejoice that that perverse individual died so ignominiously. He deserved it. I would gladly have strangled him myself if I had known the treatment he was about to inflict upon me.

And here is the list of Hertz offices near Pacific airports. San Diego (automatically excluded), Los Angeles, Santa Barbara, San Jose, Palo Alto, Oakland, San Francisco, Petaluma, Eureka, Redding, Medford, Salem, Portland (Oregon), Seattle (Washington) . . . Lots of possibilities, after all, for getting to Montreal, and I think I should delay my departure long enough for my appearance to return closer to its normal banality (I mean, no scratches, bruises, scars, wounds, and not too much volatile talcum which never stays long enough on my cheeks or chin to mask my swollen face). The Pacific coast, eroded, slashed, and tortured, suits me now, because I am like it. I too have undergone seismic shocks, landslides, tidal waves and buffetings of all sorts. The difference is that in my case a husband inflicted all my wounds. In the case of this long, unravelled coastline, an ocean did the damage. But I should take another analgesic tablet and get some sleep.

Tomorrow morning I will move again. I will leave the motel about 6:30 or 7:00 and drive up to Pasadena or Santa Monica. There, I will rent another hotel room where I will hide for 24 or 48 hours. I know too much about the murder of the druggist in San Diego; and I should take time to regain my health if I want to avoid questions by a customs officer or the airport police.

Perhaps I am healing slowly, hour by hour, but I still think the best place to fly from would be San Francisco in 2 or 3 days. Allowing time for reserving flights, let's say 4 days. I

The Antiphonary

should look better then.

The Antiphonary

(I foresee, at this point in my story, a description of Jean-William Forestier's suicide, just after his murder of the pharmacist. Such a tragic end was the only way open to Jean-William at that moment in his life, shuddering with melancholy and despair in the Hillcrest Motel.) To be written later.

(For the time being I am obsessed by my *deformis conformitas* . . .)

(A notation by Jules-César Beausang, Ed. Nagel, 1915 — *Treatise on the New Illnesses* — informs me that he never tired of re-reading the *Rhetorimachia* by Anselme de Besate, and the *De Dictamine* of Adalbert le Samaritain. To a physician like him it was perfectly normal to cultivate a style — the *conceptio,* the *oratio* and the *compositio* — for in his day scientific specialization did not involve the rigid compartmentalization that characterized it later and especially in our own era. To achieve the *congruentia* and the *cursus velox* — as opposed to the *cursus tardus* — he had to cultivate his mind and learn the different ways of putting a piece of writing together. If I can judge by the internal evidence in what I have read of Beausang, I think one can easily deduce that he liked to count himself among the "hisperic" authors — those whose books are described as making use of torrents of epithets and excessively enigmatic literary procedures. In fact, I am inclined to agree that Beausang has a manifest penchant for the grandiose, the enigmatic, and the cacozealic.)

The Antiphonary

The Septenary, by Aldem of Malmesbury, which I'm re-reading with intense fascination, reminds me of the Asianic stylistic excesses of Paracelsus and Jules-César Beausang: these bursts of virtuosity and vesperal inspiration, these spiralling arabesques and mystifying labyrinths dazzle me. Alongside this Asianic splendour, which was as prevalent among the Romans of the Hellenic period as it was among "barbarians" like Paracelsus and Beausang, the pale account of my poor existence cuts a sorry figure. I am aware of the lacks, from an Asianic point of view, in this monotonous series of events, which I am trying to transpose clearly in the language of an almost illiterate doctor. So little has happened since Jean-William's ninth fit in San Diego (except, of course, for the murder of the druggist), that I seem just to be rambling on, telling modestly what should be told with the secret and diffusive flame of love, seeking to attain the exuberant verbosity which is neither my style nor my way of being. With these words of precaution, I might say that only three weeks have passed (but three weeks!) since the preceding page. In those three weeks I have had time to leave San Modesto and Pasadena, where I stayed three full days, and finally take off from one of the runways of the international airport of San Francisco for Chicago. In Chicago I waited three long hours before catching an Air Canada plane for Montreal. I did not leave the airport during those three hours; and as I still bore some quite visible marks of the wounds Jean-William had inflicted on me I had time to re-do my makeup with base colour and mascara. In

The Antiphonary

Chicago I also tried to phone Robert Bernatchez in his office in Montreal (the firm of Lavoie, Klein and Laurin). But he wasn't in. I didn't leave a message. I had to tell myself a dozen times not to phone him at home. But this was only a temporary delay in re-establishing contact between Robert and myself. Since Drummondville we had seen each other in secret (and too briefly) but only rarely, and in sadness. These meetings, incidentally, had depressed me exceedingly. My mind was made up: I would not go to my home (as Madame Jean-William Forestier). I would stay at a hotel on my arrival in Montreal, and register, what's more, under a false name. And that is what I did. Going through customs, first American, then Canadian, I ran the first and only real risks of the whole trip (at least, those that frightened me most). I caught up with my suitcase orbiting silently on the immense mobile cone of aluminium. In a few minutes I was out of the airport building. I found a taxi and asked him to take me to the Holiday Inn on Côte de Liesse. I had the driver ask at the desk if there was a room available. I gave him my name for the clerk. He came back and informed me that there was a room reserved in my name (Madame N. Boileau, 598 King St., Sherbrooke).

It was about 9:30 in the evening. I didn't want to risk a call to Robert's apartment. I decided to wait until morning and call him at his office. I inspected my precarious make-up (soluble: by necessity). The cuts and swellings seemed better, and at least less ostentatious than they had been in San Modesto, in the motel where I cloistered myself for three whole days.

That evening (the evening of my return via Chicago to Montreal) I went to sleep on top of the bed with all my clothes on, while watching a thriller on Channel 12. I woke at dawn, surprised, looking at a little frame filled with a uniform, grey drizzle, feeble and hissing. I turned off the set, undid my dress and took a hot bath before going to bed. And slept again until 9:15.

The Antiphonary

If at this point I take the liberty of using the conventions of secondary and ternary narration, it is because I want to gain time — or rather, catch up in time with what had taken place quite outside the range of my possible knowledge. I don't know if the Asianists had a name for this type of literary procedure. Perhaps even the ancient Greek rhetors had a term for it? Is it an ellipse? Or (what do I know?) an inverted anacoluthon? The point is, all this amounts to saying that I'm about to narrate things I didn't yet know while I was in my room in the Holiday Inn Motel on Côte de Liesse. Here it is: Jean-William, having spent two days holed up in his room at the Hillcrest in San Diego, left the motel for the airport. Then, at San Diego Airport, he passed himself off at the Avis Rent-A-Car counter as if he had come from Montreal via Chicago and Los Angeles. He rented a car. From San Diego he drove east. His first stopover was Phoenix, then Denver (Colorado), then Kansas City (Kansas), then Indianapolis (Indiana) and finally, before the last leg to Montreal, Buffalo (New York State). He kept all his motel bills (including meals and frequent gin-and-tonics) which later made it possible to retrace his trajectory in detail. And all this was happening while I traversed the identical geographical distance (but by air). The evening after my arrival Jean-William got out of the car he had rented in San Diego and entered 207 d'Iberville Street in St. Lambert (our apartment house). I was not there; but Jean-William realized in a few minutes, after a brief inspection, that I had beaten him to it and emptied the place of everything that belonged to me, books, wardrobe, shoes, my personal file with photostats of my diplomas and a few securities as well. And my marriage contract with him. In fact I had called at 207 d'Iberville St. just a few hours before his arrival. Robert, keeping watch outside, stayed in his car before the front door. It was about six o'clock in the evening then. I had met Robert that very morning near his office and we had lunched together, after which he went back to his office for a few hours to look after current business. At five o'clock we were together again. He telephoned Suzanne (a trying business, I must admit) to tell her he had decided to suggest a separation arrangement on a friendly basis as soon as she was ready to discuss it. But Suzanne took a hard line, and Robert was obliged to tell her that his decision was irrevocable, he was very sorry. After 30 minutes of this conversation Robert, somewhat disarmed by Suzanne's attachment, told me what had been said; and we went off for a drink at the bar in Piazza Tomasso. He told me everything. He seemed downhearted or surprised at Suzanne's reaction. He had not foreseen this kind of problem. He told me that in any case Suzanne was going to Granby that evening to see her sister Marie-France, married and apparently happy there. They had agreed: Suzanne should take a rest of at least two days to evaluate the situation and think things over. Robert, on the phone, had been obliged to tell her everything in a rush, not sparing her feelings. That meant he had told her of our relationship (Robert's and mine). I suddenly felt ashamed before Suzanne at what I was doing. I felt a rush of friendship and affection for her, I was touched to the point of tears. My God! What a switch! Suzanne, to whom I had never given a second thought, all at once seemed invested with all the properties of femininity and gentleness. I discovered in her an uncreated image of womanhood. Poor Suzanne, poor you (I said to myself). I'm about to destroy your life, to break you forever, to steal your husband, Robert, but, you see, I love him. I know that doesn't excuse my conduct (I should say, my misconduct). I know. But I can't let that condemn me to live outside the life that belongs to me, trying in vain to find some point of attachment to Jean-William during the full bloom of his epileptic aura, trying retroactively to pardon him for the blows on my left upper lobe and the frightful kicks that ruined my viscera forever. I am gutted, all my tripes are stripped, all my fears outdistanced by events, kicked in like a poor helpless victim, covered with wounds and divers contusions — a veritable feminoid phantom straight from a car accident on highway 540, west of Dorion-sud. I came out of that pile of burning junk like a pot-roast boiled to shreds. Poor me, even more than poor Suzanne, ''I am the Rose of Sharon, the lily of the valley'' — death valley — I am the one who is supposed to be the bride of the Canticle, she whose teeth are like a flock of sheep, her breasts like two jars of melancholy. Oh! I'm sick, I'm sick at heart, and I have to go on with this story, for I'm the only one who knows its extraordinary end, its end super-multiplied in the shrubs of South San Francisco or San Mateo (just near Millbrae). May my tongue burn, as long as I possess that powerful muscle, yes, may it burn rather than reveal the truth before I'm ready, for I want to tell all, not necessarily in the order of its happening but composed in *cursus velox* (leaping to the end at the appropirate time and not without some sounds of crashing). Yes, the *cursus velox* will lead me ineluctably from Montreal to South San Francisco, then from San Mateo to San Diego and San Modesto and from Turin to Superga and Chivasso. Yes, all that and more, it's not finished, it's only beginning. I should go back now to when I was with Robert and he told me all the things he had said on the phone (Suzanne . . .) but it's getting late, and I'm falling asleep, under the euphoric and slightly neuroleptic effect of the big white and blue capsules I swallowed a few minutes ago . . . I must give in to them soon. Besides

The Antiphonary

I'm beat, absolutely exhausted. Tomorrow I'll tell the whole story, to the end, and if I have to I'll take you-know-what to keep me awake in spite of everything.

The Antiphonary

"I am the rose of Sharon, the lily of the valleys ... I am black but comely (*negra sed pulchra*)." "As the apple tree among the trees of the wood, so is my beloved among the sons ... My beloved is white and ruddy, the chiefest among ten thousand, his head is as the most fine gold, his locks are bushy and black as a raven ... he is altogether lovely ... " "Thou art all fair, my love, there is no spot in thee ... " "I am the rose of Sharon, the lily of the valleys ... "

The Antiphonary

Unable to get control of myself, I have been incapable of writing. I am in a constant panic; I don't know if I will ever be able to go on with this project before I die. It is frightful. I would not wish this terror and psychic disintegration on anyone ...

And still the days go by. I will never be able ...

The Antiphonary

Second day of lassitude. I believe that this time I've crossed the threshold of debilitation and anguish. What I most fear is my own indifference. I can feel myself cutting loose from everything . . .

"I am not the rose of Sharon, neither am I the lily of the valleys . . ."

The Antiphonary

Something is definitely wrong. Today I began cutting potatoes to make French fries. I have eaten nothing. The deep-fry is standing there. But I'm not hungry.

Relapse. My temporal vein still seems to swell noticeably at the end of the day. It has swollen several times in the last few days.

The Antiphonary

The first time I was a little surprised, but now I believe this is an unmistakable sign that I have suffered a lesion from Jean-William's blow on my temple. Alas! Every day my left temple swells until I have the impression that I am about to die of a cerebral haemorrhage. I can't go on like this, living from day to day and hoping for nothing more than to regain my health — which has been going downhill for months. This is truly sinister. I am aging rapidly and ferociously, obsessed for some reason with the days we passed at Santa Barbara, days that were premonitory (yet at the time I did not know of what) of Jean-William's ninth seizure! On the beaches of Santa Barbara I bared my body to the California sun; it gave me as it were a plethora of warmth and tan. A few days later in San Diego I grew so impregnated with sunlight that I was almost drunk with it, suddenly unable to think coldly. Yes, I am aging with frightening speed and my whole being is aimed back at those sunlit days in Santa Barbara and San Diego. You can't imagine . . . .

An entelechy, according to Aristotle and Averrhoes (*vid.* Renan, if necessary), is no longer something I possess. I am decomposing into a non-entelechy. Day after day, a "form in deformation", I go on reading and re-reading Galen, Avicenna's *Canon* (the very one burned by Theophrastus von Hohenheim in the Basel amphitheatre a few years ago — as it would have seemed to Beausang), the books of the great Alfarabi (precursor of Averrhoes and Abubacer), *The Destruction of the Philosophers* by Averrhoes, which influenced the Middle Ages as much as it did the authors of the Renaissance. *Destruction of the Destructions* (as Jorge-Luis Borges would say), that's what I should write, in the manner of the mystical quest of the great Abu'l Walid Mohammed Ibn Rosd (born in the year 520 of the Hegira in the city of Cordoba, cradle also of Maimonides, the great Jewish physician). Nothing now brings me more quickly to tears, as my discouragement grows more bitter from day to day, than to re-read authors like Alexander of Aphrodisia or Pietro Pomponazi (both disciples of the great Averrhoes), for I feel certain that I will not have time to finish this thesis which I undertook in order to change the course of my river and — also — of my will, already too intimidated by the privative choice I had made after meeting Jean-William.

But life is not necessarily a series of more or less accommodating accommodations. Nothing is less like life than some euphemistic vision of an endless negotiation with a worthwhile interlocutor. Alexander of Aphrodisia, they say, was a very elegant, seductive man, whose love-life was certainly crowded with a quantity of captivated women. In addition he managed to write the incredible series of *Disputationes* on the subject of the 6th book of Aristotle's *Physics*. And Pomponazi, for his part, was a man fatally in love with a young woman who was married to a friend of his: Lucilius Vanini, burned at the stake in 1532 (Toulouse, as we all know, was the city that burned the most: fortunate and happy city where I could wish to have been heard like Vanini uttering Lucianist theories, to have been suspected of being one, and finally to have been burned at the stake! But Pomponazi, enamoured of Clara Beltosa Vanini, was not the man to take Vanini's wife. To the end of his life he remained thus, rejected, despised, easily inclined to neurasthenia — the *mal du siècle* of the 16th century!). The very sight of Clara made him unhappy. Jules-César Beausang, as we know, had been cuckolded by his wife in Ghent and following this had fled Ghent and Flanders (the United Provinces in those days) to go up the Rhine to Strasbourg (where he visited Bucerius), then to Basel (ditto Oecolempadius, another great Reformed Church man, whom he never succeeded in counting among his friends). But Basel had become a bastion of the reformed religion (though not of Gomarism, of which Jules-César Beausang was a warm partisan but which was a sect with a pitifully small following, mainly in Bois-le-Duc and Ghent, with a few supporters in Utrecht and Antwerp, if I remember correctly). The reticence of Oecolempadius towards the man from Ghent come to visit him in Basel becomes, in the light of these facts, understandable. What could Oecolempadius do about this great doctor but turn his back on him? Alas, Jules-César Beausang — of this we are sure — felt so slighted by his behaviour that he never quite recovered from it. It is certain that in Neuchâtel — later on — poor Beausang sought no contact with Guillaume Farel, who was then the great Neuchâtel reformer in exile from France, as was also Calvin. Beausang would later have liked to make the trip to Geneva to meet Calvin (or Calvinus) who was in full power there as grand master, while in German Switzerland Zwingli (the gentlest of all, the most attractive reformer) reigned in Zurich. But alas, Zwingli met an early death at the battle of Cappel in 1531. Strangely, Jules-César Beausang seems to have had no high regard for the great reformer Zwingli. Beausang, an ardent Gomarist, remained one all his life, which, as I mentioned earlier, ended abruptly in Chivasso while he was staying in that poor inn which is mentioned in no document and has left no trace in time. Oh well! And when I went through Chivasso (with Jean-William: we were on our way to Turin) I did not recognize the Via Santa Clara nor the inn where Jules-César Beausang knew the pangs of his death-agony. In Turin, however, I do remember seeing the church of San Fernando sopra San Tomaso (a modern church built on the ancient foundation of the parish church of San Tomaso), as well as the oldest part of the great modern city (the quarter of Borgo Santo Spirito) where, according to the best guesses of our historians, the market was held at which poor Renata one day met her friend Rosalita. Jean-William, of course, had only one desire: to go up along the Sesia (my sweet and gentle Sesia) to Modena, with the idea of visiting the Ferrari factory. But our time was too short, and Jean-William had to give up this excursion to Modena and instead take the train (*direttissimo*) for Rome, via Genoa, Pisa, Civita Vecchia and (*doppo*) Roma. Those were the good days of our marriage. I was in perfect form for working at my thesis. Since then Santa Barbara intervened (sunlit but clouded) and, above all, San Diego and the pharmacist (Mister Gordon, murdered in cold blood — if I may say so — by a jealous husband come all the way from Montreal to perpetrate his crime which I saw with my own eyes, saw it . . .).

The Borgo San Sepulcro in Turin I visited as well. It is a tiny neighbourhood, antique and sad, filled with slums. It seems to emanate (by pure and simple emanationism) from the 16th century. I also recall "La Fortezza," the ruined prison on the road to Superga (we had rented a Fiat 124 for excursions). It was a somber souvenir for me, for poor Renata Belmissieri was unjustly executed there (denounced by the lovely Antonella with the complicity of Leonico Chigi). I would have liked to pay my last respects to the cemetery of Santa Croce, for it held the remains of the few noble or respectable victims of the pandemic that swept Chivasso in 1536. To be sure there is nothing to see in Santa Croce but a common ditch, surmounted by a monument created by an anonymous artist of the period. But time was lacking. There is never time enough to grow old peacefully, to convalesce, to strike back at our attackers (sparing them a more sordid death), to write a thesis which is destined — forever — to remain a hypothesis about the "medical science" of the 16th century. I shall never finish this thesis! Others, in the mean-

time, have taken advantage of me, beaten me, raped me, killed
me a thousand times, beaten me again, slapped me with the
back of their hand or engulfed me in sadness (for I am utterly
lacking in any "impetus" toward rebirth) in which I swim without
surfacing. I am sinking. In this filthy and polluted water I defy
any woman to succeed better than I do. My God, it is unlivable,
unbearable, intolerable, lethal! I never knew that I was born
for this superbly interrupted career, now ruined, of philosopher
of sciences — or thinker (philosopher . . . thinker — I love
words that have no feminine form).

No doubt about it, the story I undertook in Santa Barbara
carries me well beyond my field. I am no longer moving on
solid ground, given my academic qualifications (MD, 2nd cycle),
given, also, my personal orientation in medicine (and in philosophy and the history of science), given, as well, my heart,
which has been in rags for a certain time now, following events
that I can transcribe only with great difficulty and effort, not
of will-power, for I have none, but simply the effort required
(on getting up in the morning) to inject myself with an overdose
of racemic acid (not to be confused with morituric acid). But
I'm already nearing the end of my course, on the point of adjourn-
ing *sine die* my everyday experience (calvary would be more
accurate, but too christophoric). The lines I write today (and
under what conditions!) have cost me 88c worth of acid and
a few hours of my time (but my time is no longer a cost factor).
To which we must add the bill for 58c which I will incur, before
sleeping, for barbiturates and soporifics (mixed, of course). Not
exorbitant, as you can see. The trouble is that I must finish
this process as quickly as possible or I risk leaving this vale
of tears for a better world with no more warning than Jean-William
gave the druggist in San Diego before he drilled him with a
bullet from his .45 police special.

The Antiphonary

Renata Belmissieri died by hanging in Superga. A few days later (2 or 3), Antonella and Leonico Chigi fled (he disguised as a layman) toward the Swiss border, which they crossed north of Domodossola. Then they crossed the Simplon Pass and stopped at the summit to spend their first nuptial night (if one may use the expression). The story of this voyage, and of the first night the abbot Leonico Chigi spent in Antonella's arms, is transmitted to us in the book he himself published under the name of a certain Jules-César Beausang, an illustrious physician and audacious thinker of the Renaissance and Reformation. Chigi, imitating the majestic periods of Beausang, integrated his own story into the work thus adulterated. It was not the story of a defrocked ex-priest running away with a manuscript stolen from a girl about to be hanged (Renata), but that of a poor widower who, after a monstrously troubling episode with this murderess who was taken by the Turin police and hanged, came in contact with Mrs Zimara, a respectable widow in difficulties with the Piedmontese police following the death of her husband the printer, for the late Mr Zimara had been a publisher of works forbidden in France and other Catholic realms, which works he then re-sold as contraband beyond the borders. Beausang — at least this is the version in the book — disguised himself as a priest to be able to circulate freely in Turin, meet his contacts and settle Mrs Zimara's heritage, after which he exchanged his robes for layman's clothing and left on a second honeymoon with Antonella Zimara. Beausang intended to support his pretty young wife with the sums he would receive from the sale of his book, or rather, this manuscript. His name, moreover, gave him access to the printers of Switzerland and perhaps even those of France, some of whom, it was said at the time, had all the audacity of heretics without joining them: Vascosan, Jean de Catuce, Claude Baduel, Sebastian Gryphe (most of them established in Lyon) — all famous names at that time, taking their places only after those of Boniface Amerbach (of Basel), Aldo Manuce (the Venetian to whom we owe the invention of italics), or Josse Bade (from Ghent). Beausang-Chigi knew the reputation of all these men, and now that he had run away with Antonella over the Alps he dreamed of nothing but finding work — if only as a proof-reader — in one of those great printing houses. He could also, of course, translate foreign works (from Italian to French, from Dutch to French, from Latin to French, from Greek to Latin . . .).

After their first night in the Albergo del Sempione, right on the plain where an Alpine lake creates a wild setting between two mountain crests, Antonella and Chigi-Beausang went down to Brig in a spectacular storm which had blown up from the Rhone valley into the secret folds and corners of the Simplon range. When they reached Brig — a charming town that Beausang knew but which Chigi (his double) now saw with ecstasy for the first time — they found the place so attractive that they decided to stay a few days. Leonico Chigi-Beausang had fallen madly in love with the young widow, whom he discovered in all her splendour as the couple retired together at the end of the day. A veritable second youth — the first for Chigi — was this period of Beausang's amorous exaltation. He could not find enough words of praise for her; he was quite under the spell of her physical beauty, her strength, her maturity, her physical plenitude (I think of Antonella as a ''strong girl,'' as some put it to describe this kind of non-thinness), the naked beauty of her breasts, the curve of her legs, the few ''water-marks'' from

103

her only childbirth (a girl who died at the age of three months), the interest she took in the intellectual preoccupations of Beausang-Chigi (we can imagine Chigi, when the couple were in bed, reading, in the evening, the stolen manuscript by Jules-César Beausang, and Antonella yawning and dropping off to sleep), her taste for play, her passion for the poor (suspicious, don't you think?). Already during their stay in Brig she would enquire where the poor quarter of town was, and in the evening at the supper-hour she would go to that part of town, encourage the good people (the poor), distribute a few provisions that she herself had bought at the market of Brig, sometimes even a little wine from Valais (at 5 sols the bottle). These do-gooding, charitable excursions finally annoyed Chigi somewhat, alone and bored in his room. At last one night Antonella came back exceptionally late from her visit to the poor. Chigi-Beausang went to sleep before her return (doubtless reading his manuscript).

But in the morning, at dawn, he awoke fresh as a rose before Antonella had even opened an eye. Then he saw on her skirt (for she had gone to bed with all her clothes on) red stains spattered on the bib (nowadays we would say the apron) and near her neck and around her breasts. Chigi, worried, wondered what these stains could be. But the answer came — without warning — from the vinous breath of his companion. She had drunk too much — *really* too much. It would seem, the young priest must have said to himself, that frequenting those of low habits brings about a kind of contagion (a Beausang word which he had no doubt picked up from the vocabulary of the great doctor whose reincarnation he aspired to become). He nursed his companion for hours, until she had vomited everything left in her stomach. This way, said Chigi to himself, she has had her lesson. As a result I have no need to lecture her . . .

That day Antonella stayed in bed, silent, perhaps a little apprehensive. But Chigi had prepared everything for their depar-

ture toward Sion. The Brig-Lausanne diligence rolled off after
dinner and drove all night until its stop in Lausanne. The change
of horses was made in Sierre, where the passengers stretched
their legs a bit and had a snack in a little restaurant that stayed
open for their benefit. In Sion the false abbot and the young
widow (who had left off her mourning and slept through the
whole trip) stopped at the Hotel des Etrangers, in the rue Tour-
billon, number 8. The diligence always stopped at this hotel
to leave or take on its travellers. The inn was simple but very
cosy. The couple took a room facing the castle of Sion (which
is down in the valley), and with the help of porters brought
up the many pieces of baggage they had with them. The priest
from Turin carried Beausang's manuscript under his arm.

Their stay in Sion, a splendid medieval town, was shorter
than in Brig. After one day and one night the couple, weary,
again caught the diligence for Lausanne, then, after a night in
Lausanne, went without stopover to Geneva.

The Antiphonary

The move was made, a few days after we had found each other
again, to Robert's apartment on Maisonneuve Street (a 12-storey
building). At last I was somewhere. During the whole time that
I had been dragging my books and files about with me, with
my troubles as high as your nose and my dresses all rumpled
and crushed, I had longed to park these things somewhere.
Suzanne had left the place, lock, stock and barrel. She had left
a few days ago, as a matter of fact. You could smell it. There
was nothing in the bedroom closets, nothing in the drawers,
nothing a woman would use in the bathroom, not a fancy comb
or a curler, not a pair of tweezers, nothing. I was shaken. She
had even taken a few books from the shelves in the living-room
and one or two pictures her mother had given her as engagement
presents. I came as a stranger into this apartment which belonged
to Suzanne and Robert.

"It doesn't bother you, I hope?"

"No," I said to Robert. "Well, of course, for a second I
felt a little strange. But really it doesn't bother me. After all,
it's inevitable in a way that Suzanne should make herself felt
in this building, in this apartment. You can't do anything about
it, and neither can I."

"Just as soon as I have the money," Robert said, "we'll
find a new place. In a month or two at the most. Till then we
just have to get used to this one. Especially as I have to pay
alimony to Suzanne for a while. My partner advised me strongly
to do something of the sort."

106

The Antiphonary

"Anyway, the main thing is to make sure she doesn't turn up here."

"Oh, Suzanne isn't like that."

"I'll take your word for it."

And we kissed.

I was not too well that day. And everything Robert had told me a few days before — about what had happened in St. Lambert and what Jean-William had done since I left him in San Diego — haunted me still. I was prey to a phantasmagoria of fears and terrors. And I still had two great bruises on my left thigh which I had been unable to hide from Robert.

After Robert left for his office in the morning I was frightened at the slightest noise in the apartment. I arranged my books on the shelves of Robert's library (he had only books on law and diplomatic history). My most precious ones came first (Arnold de Villeneuve, Beausang, Gilles de Corbeil, Guy de Chauliac, and so on: Alfarabi, Avicenna, Averrhoes, Abubacer — my favourite Arabs — Jerome Fabrice d'Acquapendente, Gabriel Fallope, Fracastoro and all the others. It somehow did me good just to handle these books, all of which reminded me of the thesis I had undertaken and interrupted, but which I wanted to continue and finish by the next fall term. When I saw beneath my very eyes the books of Mussa Brassavole and Ulrich von Hutten, Valescus of Trent and John of Gaddesden, I felt as if I had been invested with a renewed, unwritten mandate to end this long work of exhumation and elucidation I had begun. Yet the moment I laid hand on a copy of the books (genuine or adulterated) of Beausang, I felt a frightful shock. I saw Santa Barbara again, and San Diego, and that Hillcrest Motel I had left so gladly, the dark pharmacy where I was drugged, but with no ill effects (one thing is sure, I told myself: Robert must never hear of that). God, how much horror I had accumulated in me, what frightful, unforgettable scenes!

The Antiphonary

After a few days of this little life I again fell into the routine that was my lot: I worked, without enthusiasm, I re-read my notes and my favourite authors, I prepared a meal for Robert's return (about 5:30 in the afternoon). In fact I was extremely bored, but I didn't want to complain to Robert, or to anyone. After all, I deserved my fate. What was more, I could count myself lucky not to be worse off!

One day around 3:30 in the afternoon Robert turned up. I was on the bed doing nothing but having a good sleep. He frightened me so that I screamed with all my might. But I recognized him at once, and my first terror ebbed away and disappeared. Robert had come with the surprise that we were going to take a few days holiday outside Montreal. I flew to his arms, I was so pleased for once to leave that apartment where I spent my days with such difficulty waiting for Robert.

"Leaving right now?" I asked.

"Right now," he said. "We're off. Quick, throw a few things in a bag, a few shirts, a few dresses — not too much stuff — some books and our bathing suits."

"I'll be ready in ten minutes," I told him. "You can gather your shaving things while I pack, and change if you want to."

(I asked no more questions. I was exultant as a child when school is let out early.)

"But Robert, why today? Why did you decide to leave, just like that?"

"I was fed up with the office, and anyway I think we've earned these few days, don't you?"

"Oh yes! But where are we going?"

"Where would you like to go? Our only limitation is that I have to be at work Monday morning. That leaves us four whole days, four and a half."

"That's perfect! Four and a half days, that's terrific, don't you think?"

The Antiphonary

"Yes, my darling. But be quick, now. I give you fifteen minutes to have everything in the car, or you're in real trouble."

"I'll make it, don't worry. I'll be ready in a flash."

Well, after a few small delays we did get away in Robert's Rambler. Supposedly we were going nowhere in particular, but actually it was agreed that we should spend these 4 days of holiday in Magog, at the Auberge de l'Etoile (and if there should be no room, at the Auberge de la Lanterne, between Magog and Georgeville). This was perfect for me for I knew the area only from having been through it once or twice as a child with my parents and sisters. The same went for Robert; he had been through Magog only once when he was 14 or 15. Thus the place had no associations, neither for me nor for Robert. It was almost ideal. At the Etoile Motel, just north of that immense lake which at its southern end wets the soil of the U.S.A., I changed from my travelling dress to my bathing suit to bask in the sun of this fine afternoon. The room opened onto a lawn where two folding chairs allowed us to sun ourselves. In May the sun was already warm. I should add that May had been exceptionally hot in Montreal. Robert did the same. It was already almost 5 but the sunlight was still strong. The public swarmed down to the lake-front before us, on the other side of Highway 1. It was really very pleasant.

That evening, around 7, we went to the motel restaurant, a very proper place with delicious cuisine which was, for me, a welcome respite from my daily task. Robert ordered red wine, a Valpolicella, to go with the rumpsteak we had ordered. Then after dinner, as we were unpacking our things, Robert asked me, very casually:

"Tell me, isn't it about time for your period?"

"Just a second, I'll look in my little book. I always make a note of it. Here we are ... Why, by the way? Are you worried?"

The Antiphonary

"No, but ... I don't know. I'd rather be sure."

"Sure of what?"

I felt the earth slipping away from under my feet. I saw a little cross in my calendar, and it was three days ago.

"Christine, what's happening? You've gone white! What's the matter?"

"I'm pregnant by Jean-William."

When I'd said it I crumpled into an armchair. Robert was very kind and attentive, most considerate. He treated me like a pitiful patient.

"Oh," I went on, "I'm pregnant by him, no doubt of it. Here, look at my calendar. I was supposed to have my period three days ago. And I never miss ... See here, my dangerous time coincides with the end of my stay in San Diego ... Just a little oversight!"

(I knew very well that I was pregnant not by Jean-William but by the druggist in San Diego. I thought of the atrocious and impossible position I had put Robert in by this brutal announcement. And even at that my lie protected me from revealing the full extent of the scandal and horror ... The business in the drugstore, at night, with a stranger, a stranger called Gordon ...)

Silence grew between Robert and me. I could say nothing more. I might as well, I thought, play the part of a victim of fate, a poor girl in trouble. But it was unforgivable, really unforgivable.

"What are you thinking, Robert?"

(I was standing close beside him. He was watching night descend on Lake Memphramagog.)

"I don't know ... "

"Are you angry with me?" I asked, sniffling.

"Yes, Christine, I am," he said coldly, turning and staring at me.

The Antiphonary

I couldn't bear to meet his eyes, and I could neither take on his pain nor cure it. No more could I excuse my own behaviour. But good God, is it my fault if I was raped by a druggist who took advantage of my sorry plight and my suffering body? (But how could I tell that to Robert? After all, it was not for him to bear the weight of my sins for me, especially not that one. And I still remembered a frightful scene between us in a Drummondville motel.)

"I am angry with you Christine, I am, I am, and I don't believe I will ever stop resenting you for this. You had no right to do it to me."

"But I didn't do it to you, as you say. It's not my fault, you know. Truly. It was the situation I described to you, in San Diego, between Jean-William and me."

"But you didn't tell me that part. I'd have remembered, I'm sure. You told me about his fit. But I suppose that was another part of the fit, taking you by force and giving you a baby."

"You're right, Robert." (I was crying.) "I was wrong to want to spare you a scene that was a nightmare for me. You're right. I've done you a terrible wrong. Can you forgive me?"

Time passed slowly. Robert remained at the window watching the mountains disappear across that invisible border, far away. And I, curled on the bed, cried without shedding tears. It was as if I were dried out, but conscious that I had brought misfortune to Robert, making him leave Suzanne for me. After minutes that seemed endless he said:

"Very well. The child will be ours. I accept it because I love you ... Christine!"

And he threw himself on me, crazed and passionate as I had never seen him, stripping off my clothes with irresistible haste and desire, all multiplied by this baby (from a stranger, since dead) which I bore in my womb in an embryonic state. He was all in a sweat, uncontrollable, almost violent with the wild current of his desire bearing him toward me. And his climax came with loud cries, long before I began to come (by rubbing against him) after he had poured his soul into my body.

"I love you, Christine, I love you. And I'll gladly accept this child if you want to have it ... I already feel that I want it, I'm sure I will love it ... I am sure I'll always love you, never doubt that."

This was how he talked to me, later in the evening when he awoke, still lying on me, still fully erect inside me. He had never been so astonishing. I couldn't help massaging his penis with my muscles, moving up and down, and by vaginal constriction pressing his flaming symbol of flesh within me. I was iridescent with his fire. He had slept like that. But I had lain with open eyes, unable to sleep, stunned by the very thought that the father of my child was a faceless druggist from San Diego who had met an ignoble death. There was a nightmare quality about it. My God, I had lived through it all! And I had seen with my own eyes, *seen*, the druggist fall behind his counter after having received two bullets (official version in the San Diego Telegraph) from Jean-William Forestier, my husband.

Robert pulled me out of bed (and I was still naked) by the hand and picked up the phone. He ordered two gin-and-tonics for room 17 — specifying "Tanqueray, not Gordon's" which made me shiver. Then he hung up and said:

"Get dressed, beautiful. The waitress will be here in two minutes. Here, take some money." (He fumbled in his pocket and tossed a $5 bill on the bed.)

I did my best to scramble into a dress, with no bra or panties. Then I quickly pulled a woollen sweater over my dress, which I had no time to zip in the back. Robert was running his bath.

After a few seconds (lightening service) there was a knock at the door. A young girl, prettily dressed in a costume of the canton of Valais, was there with ice and a bottle of Schweppes.

The Antiphonary

I gave her the $5 and she made change while I placed the tray right beside me, under the TV set. I gave her a 25-cent tip and she left, apparently satisfied.

"Come here, Christine. I'm in the bath. There's room for two."

"Just a second."

I took off the things I had pulled on for the waitress' benefit and walked naked into the bathroom. Robert was luxuriating in the tub, relaxed, contented in the water which he had turned blue with an overdose of bubble-bath. I could barely see him for bubbles.

"Come in," he said. "It's great."

(And in fact I found this bath, prepared by Robert, particularly good and restful, and his caresses under the water still more divine. I was totally excited by his innumerable caresses and touches. I let it all happen. And after a time I was surprised to hear myself crying aloud with my climax which Robert had provoked. And suddenly I was quite weak.)

"But what about you?" I asked.

"Don't worry. I'll come in you a bit later if you still want it."

I found him marvellous that evening, full of love, overflowing with gentleness and consideration. I discovered him with astonishment, and was happy to have chosen him. With him I would re-make my life. Of that I was now certain.

The Antiphonary

My sadness knows no bounds. When I evoke those moments, those fractions of time that we lived in Magog in the Etoile Motel, my eyes are wet and flooded with tears — as they are now. No bounds, indeed; my sadness knows no bounds, it is measureless, endless, bottomless and irreversible. The more I sink into it the less possible it is to extricate myself. My sadness is a veritable quicksand, viscous and soft . . . in my own image.

"O pulcherrima mulierum, o bene dicta inter mulieres, cujus pulchritudo benedictio est, cujus pulchritudo ipse benedictus fructus ventris tui est," as Rupert of Deutz said, a monk in Liege. And he went on: *"O pulchritudo admirabilis quam sic admiratur septem praeconiis. Consideravit oculos, capillos, dentes, labia, genas, collum et ubera et pro singulis dilectus singula cantavit dignae collaudationis capitula. Hic sunt dulces moduli musicae coelestis . . . "*

What a dazzling description of the woman I am not and will never be again. There's an end to my beauty, for, as St. Thomas said, the beauty of woman is twofold: *"Prima est claritas, secunda est caritas,"* managing a touching fit of word play. "Thou art beautiful in thy works and thy simplicity, beautiful in act and in life, beautiful in thy knowledge and in thy body through taming the flesh and its voluptuousness, and in thy soul in extirpating to the root all desires of this world, beautiful in the flesh and in chastity, beautiful in spirit through love, beautiful in secret and in public, beautiful in gentleness and beautiful in combat." (Thomas Gallo of Verceuil).

The Antiphonary

I, of course, am beautiful neither in my flesh, nor in secret, nor in my body nor through chastity. All these cistercian connotations of woman's beauty are denied me. I know it all too well; I am saddened by it. I could die of it. I am in constant agony, I feel myself caught in the moving and viscous sand that for me takes the place of solid ground.

In Magog I saw Robert wildly happy, excited, unable to control his febrility and his obsessional fury. In Magog everything went off splendidly, after that dry conversation between him (at the window) and myself (lying on the bed). He threw himself savagely on the bed where I was and undressed me murmuring incomprehensible (or inaudible) phrases while I let him do what he liked with me, though I was disconcerted and almost frightened by his state of exaltation. You'd think the announcement of my (future) baby had suddenly incited him like a pointed spur. He rolled me on the bed and pushed me around to get my clothes off. Strangely enough, he did not even notice that I let him have his way. "The beauty of the breasts," said Vincent of Beauvais, "lies in a happy medium between protruding opulence and flatness in volume" — "*quasi repressa sed non depressa, leniter restricta, non fluitantia licenter.*" Thus my breasts, exuberant but relaxed (like myself), spilled beyond their lingerie sheath, while Robert, precise but obsessed, slipped off my underpants with the grey-pink lace fringe. I was, as it were, on display beneath him, though he did not see from a proper Vasarian perspective. My breasts hung down, I was breathing hard, my body still hurt, but I could not escape the embrace of my lover. He was pressed against me, almost buried in my underthings, between my breasts. He had no thought for appearances — and I had no appearances left. I was all yielding, with not a single invulnerable surface for him to touch, unable to restrain my moans when he massaged me everywhere at once, sucking my nipples, pressing my sides, crushing with all his weight my vain and banal beauty,

115

all at once infusing into it violently — all the slippery fluidity
of his belly. Oh, heaven! Why am I not beautiful? — but in
the sense the Aquinate would have wished: full of *claritas* but
also of *caritas*! There is no joy without love, Saint Bonaventure
said. Thomas Gallo de Verceuil said rightly that the enjoyment
of beauty was a kind of sinking into passivity. There it is! How
I understand his expression! Ecstasy, passivity, receptivity:
pregestaltic form of the langorous liquefaction of love's pleasure
. . .

But that's no longer real. My sadness outruns my pleasure,
cancels it out. Totalitarian rebuttal, my sadness wipes out everything in its path: memory, joys, brief ecstasies, other venereal
delectations, the preambles, paraphrases, long, supple, declara-
tory caresses, the advances, the indecent fingering . . . "Magog"
remains for me the morose designation of the most beautiful
point in my poor existence. The previous years, weeks, months,
the horrible days in San Diego, the vague glimmers of memory
of the little dispensary of a certain pharmacist, all pales beside
that single period of exploding and overflowing love. I was
covered with it, inseminated, sponge-like, viscous, shifting as
the sands of sadness, soaked, drenched with this vital liquid
that came to feed me — but all in vain . . . How can I say
it? I no longer knew what to do with such a syntagmatic flood
of sperm! Oh, I would say to myself, I won't come tonight.
Another time. But no, I would rub obstinately against the teetering
body of Robert, seeking my own death in a final spasm (torn
from God-knows-what inner hiding-place).

This was more than pleasure. It was my war-cry. Yes, all
the dikes blew out at once, flooding the lower and temporal
veins of my fevered body with a new sea! Oh, I had forgotten
how cool those waves were! Holland was drowned, me too in
my seminal haemorrhage. I lost consciousness. And when I
knew again where I was (too soon, alas), when I returned from

my voyage to the centre of the earth, I saw Robert — above my face — sleeping deeply, snoring with relief and relaxation. His (unconscious happiness seemed to me the reward I had not deserved. *Infusio caritatis*, as Marsilio Ficino would have said — and did in fact say in black and white, in his *DE VOLUPTATE*.

The Antiphonary

After Sion (I explained to Robert as we lay in bed in his apartment), Chigi-Beausang went to Lausanne where the couple spent the night, and at dawn next day they went on to Geneva. This last leg along the northwest shore of Lake Leman was a short one. At that time you could travel from Lausanne to Geneva (Genf, in German) in eight or ten hours, according to the multivariable factors of the state ot the roads, the weather, and the energy of the horses (four of them) pulling the diligence. Antonella and Leonico Chigi-Beausang entered Geneva by the quarter of les Pâquis, the post-diligence rattling along at a great rate. Then, both of them in raptures over the sight of Mont Blanc (which for them was called Monte Rosa) thrusting up into the landscape, they were brought to the Hôtel des Baillis, rue du Chapitre, 17 (near the cathedral). The year 1536 was one of celebration for the Genevans. They had reconquered their dignity (which had been under the tutelage of the Duke of Savoie until 1535) and opted, in 1535, for the reformed religion as preached by Calvin, the ''French'' reformer, as he was then called. In 1536 the *Christian Institution* appeared in Latin, then in a popular French edition. Guillaume Farel had exhorted Calvin to stay in Geneva that very year, to train preachers and give catechism lessons. Geneva, in that year of 1536, became the ''model'' reformed church.

The sermons of the young Calvin (27 years old) were heard and repeated through the whole city of Geneva (a Republic, the Genevans called it). Calvin, at the very heart of European

118

commercial activity, inveighed against the useless luxury of the merchants and their "swinish self-indulgence". Calvin was not only bishop of this reformed religion, he became the First Citizen of Geneva (thus combining two powers that Julius Caesar had held in his day). There was a state of martial law (which the rough Calvin loved). Laws against any citizen taken in a state if inebriation, laws against the theatre, against strolling players, against citizens failing to go to church, against adultery.

Chigi-Beausang quickly saw which way the wind was blowing. He and Antonella needed only to lie with confidence about their marital status and — as soon as possible — announce themselves as adherents of the new faith. For this purpose there had to be an act of public abjuration before a pastor of the church.

After wandering in the streets of the Corraterie and on the Place St -Pierre, Leonico Chigi (alias Beausang) was obliged as soon as possible to make contact with those close to the great man, Calvin, bringing recommendations from a pastor who was "persona grata" (in Calvin's eyes) to whom he would offer his official abjuration and that of his legal spouse, Antonella. He was referred to a certain Jérôme Bolsec. But Chigi was out of luck. In the meantime Bolsec had been arrested and thrown in irons for having publicly criticized Calvin's doctrine of predestination. Bolsec barely escaped execution. Chigi, after this vain attempt, tried another Protestant (a preacher this time): François Favre. A short time after, François Favre was hauled into court along with his concubine, the wife of a certain Ami Perrin. The sentence was severe and highly deterrent: the two were banished from Geneva. Chigi and Antonella trembled for their safety.

Every night Leonico Chigi (alias Beausang) put all this down on paper (but using a mirror so that his writing could not be deciphered). The couple lived in a small lodging near the Corraterie. It was cramped, but enough for their needs at the time. No wine at table (unlike Turin), no showy excursions, no fine clothes. Leonico and Antonella lived on Antonella's heritage, eating regularly into her capital.

A few months later nothing was left. Leonico, idle until now, had to look for work, some occupation — at the risk, however, of submitting to the numerous depredations of the tax collector of the Republic of Geneva. In the evenings, in bed, the former abbot from Turin read Antonella passages from Jules-César Beausang, and some of his own composition (the very ones which for us form the framework of Beausang's prose). A life of luxury and idleness seemed to him the ultimate in happiness. Chigi had never felt so free. He had no desire to perform menial tasks in a printer's shop. Antonella, for her part, had scarcely worked in her life. Idleness seemed a normal thing to her.

"This couple," I explained to Robert, "led a heavenly life. For the former abbot and the young widow it was like the pleasant aimlessness of Adam's life with Eve in their terrestrial paradise."

In fact (and I know that Robert accuses me of extrapolating) the couple felt themselves on the margin of a rigid society, inquisitorial, strongly (and roughly) organized and policed. It couldn't go on forever. Antonella and Chigi were both running out of lies to tell. They did not know how to explain their disproportionate and suspect leisure.

It seems (at least I believe this to be so) that Antonella found the situation particularly hard to take. She, in contrast to her supposed husband, learned to speak the French of the inhabitants of Geneva almost without accent. But she could stand no more of this monotonous, dull, unbearable, marginal existence. At heart she wished for acceptance by a society that Chigi, for his part, condemned or feared. In any case, in 1537 (in the month of February) we find in the papers of Chigi-Beausang mention of certain absences on the part of his young wife Antonella. In fact, when we examine the texts closely we find her absent almost every evening. One night she came back from

120

work (Antonella said: work at the central market) on the stroke
of midnight. Chigi awakened by the twelve strokes of the cathedral
clock, saw her staggering in. He was most upset, and a scene
ensued between them. But the neighbours began to protest at
the noise and say things like "dirty Italians," so that the couple
had to lower their voices. Antonella undressed, but Chigi,
thoroughly awake, did not want to go back to bed. She did
her best to lead him on: she showed herself almost naked just
before slipping between the sheets. Chigi, unmoved at first, could
not resist for long. But strange to say (at least, this is how he
tells it), Chigi thought he had suddenly become impotent. He
could not achieve sufficient rigidity to enter Antonella. He was
soft and seemingly petrified by impotence, truly paralyzed in
his virile member, unable to give it even a minimal consistency
for purposes of copulation with Antonella. Humiliated by this
incident, which he was utterly unable to explain, Leonico Chigi
had to be satisfied with the physical warmth of his partner, who,
once in bed, lost no time in falling asleep. Poor Chigi, he was
sleeping beside his companion, but abandoned — how abandoned!
— to his own solitude and impotence. This interlude ended in
desolation and sadness and in the intolerable silence of the Gene-
van night. After twelve this silence grew heavy, for noisemakers
incurred punishments out of all proportion to their offence. If
they were foreigners, moreover, they risked being simply pushed
across the Republic's borders — like some citizen who had committed fiscal fraud or buried himself in debts.

The Antiphonary

I spent hours and evenings recounting all this (the adventures of Chigi and Antonella) to Robert. But I wonder if I really captured his interest with all the vague theories advanced in the *Paraminum* or the *Paragranum*, the lyric elucubrations of the *Christian Institution* or the cynical jokes in the *Christian Destitution* (by Michel Servet) or the *Christianismo Restitutio (idem)*. I really cannot tell. I know only that this kind of story-telling, which I began simply to give Robert some relief from his law files, brought great excitement for me, especially in re-creating the atmosphere of the period, the dramatic experiences of the plagiarist, Chigi, and Antonella's peccadillos. I was carried away with all these things, they seemed to me a kind of triumph, I can't say exactly why.

"And you," said Robert, "how are you these days?"

"Oh fine. Why are you looking at me like that?"

"I was thinking about . . . your baby."

"Oh, yes . . . well, everything's fine!"

"And when is the happy day?" Robert asked.

"Nine months . . . Just a second, I have to count. One, two, three . . ." (the rest in silence) " . . . the 25th of December this year. Or maybe New Year's day."

(I had lost my impetus. Not that this reminder of my pregnancy bothered me, but Robert was beginning to look like a thundercloud. He looked more and more depressed, and I didn't know what to do about it.)

"What about the doctor? Have you chosen your maternity

doctor?'' (Robert was staring at me severely, darkly.)

"No,'' I said, "I hadn't thought about it yet. What about you? Don't you have any obstetrician friends? Somebody you know, that you could recommend?''

(Our evening was starting badly, or was going to finish badly. I tried to rescue the situation by going back to my couple in Geneva, Chigi and Antonella.)

"You know,'' I said, "when Leonico Chigi and Antonella started arguing in Geneva, their neighbours gave them a great deal of trouble. In one night they lost the confidence of their landlord, who was from Zurich and extremely rich.''

"And what about the manuscript?'' His question was posed without much conviction. Behind it I sensed that something had come seriously undone.

"Jules-César Beausang's manuscript?'' I asked.

"Yes,'' said Robert, "that's the one. What happened to it?''

"Well, as I told you, abbot Chigi, freshly defrocked, usurped the identity of the author, that famous old doctor from Ghent. And after long and sterile negotiations with Tronchin, a printer in Geneva, and Diodati, the famous bookseller (and Calvin's delegate to the synod of Dordrecht), Chigi realized that he wasn't going to make his fortune in Geneva. He then heard of a certain Guillaume Cop (at least the Chigi-Beausang text tells us so) who was a printer in Basel and a friend of Guillaume Budé, printer-publisher in Lyon. But the distance between Geneva and Basel was just as great as that which separated the Republic from Lyon. It was a simple question of money, and our couple, Antonella and Leonico, were beginning to feel the pinch. Antonella worked evenings unloading wagons of foodstuffs at the market to keep them alive.''

(We may may be excused for thinking that Antonella did more than unload carts of fruit and vegetables, that indeed she offered her services on the street at a high price. She must, in fact, have done so systematically, for Chigi and Antonella seem to have had no serious financial problems during their stay in Geneva. Yet Antonella's inheritance must have melted away after the couple left Turin. The episode of Antonella's late homecoming gives us certain strong circumstantial clues in this connection.)

"Do you believe that stuff Antonella told Chigi when she got home from 'work' around midnight? A bit fishy, isn't it?"

"Oh, I really don't know. I'm too close to the manuscript, you know, I'm living in it, and I can't back off and judge fairly. Frankly, Antonella doesn't seem too trustworthy to me," I said to Robert, "but to go as far as calling her a sidewalk pro ... "

"Come on," said Robert. "Admit it's a little funny when she comes home at midnight with wine-spots on her bib."

"Yes," I replied, "I suppose you're right." (It bothered me, I don't know why, to accuse Antonella of becoming a streetwalker to obtain the money to keep Chigi. And I thought Robert was up to something. His questions seemed tendentious to me. I thought he was trying, behind this screen of supposedly neutral interrogations, to put down Antonella, in a way he would never admit — and with her everything that was feminine about me, my past, all the memories I had already shared with him in Drummondville.)

"Well," Robert went on, "if you find her suspect you might as well be logical and admit that Antonella Zimara's behaviour was the cover for something remarkably like old-fashioned prostitution!"

"Do you think so?" I asked, with false naivete. "Do you really think she was capable of such hypocrisy, and of such a degrading activity?"

"I don't know, Christine. You should know that *yourself,* it seems to me," said Robert.

I became aggressive.

"Do you know," I said, "I think it would suit you perfectly

if Antonella Zimara had been a whore in Geneva. That one little detail is obviously more important to you than all the rest. You seem to have a furious desire to prove that Antonella was the worst kind of slut. I'm right, aren't I? Say it! Don't be polite. Politeness never bothered you before. You've said a few things to me already. I know the old song. Just go right ahead."

"To what do you refer?"

(Robert spoke coldly to me. A glacial distance had suddenly established itself between us. I felt that his attitude had changed, that in fact he was barely restraining his anger or his contempt. Another word would have brought the explosion and he'd have turned into the prosecutor, as he did so well in Drummondville just before the political meeting in the Civic Centre when I was so furious at Jean-William. And now I didn't have too good control of my reactions. I was already in tears, unable to squeeze out a word, let alone a sentence. I was condemned to silence, nailed to the spot by his disdainful, haughty, aggressive attitude.)

Antonella and her behaviour, her evening job that ran into night hours and her supposed ill-conduct, all served as pretexts for Robert to ruin things and transfer his contempt to me, accusing me indirectly. That night (in a rage) I threw the book across our bedroom (where Suzanne had slept before my arrival). I turned resolutely to the wall, in silence, not saying a word, suddenly full of hate because Robert had — really — laid a trap for me and I had fallen into it head first. I couldn't turn toward him. I waited until he put out his bedside lamp, which he did around midnight after flipping through some American magazines he always kept there. When it was dark I managed to get my nerves under control. But I found a position where I was not even aware of his body. It took me quite a while to go to sleep. I insulted him silently, to myself, and cursed him for spoiling my bedtime in this way and also for having made me hate the (otherwise fascinating) story of Chigi and Antonella.

The Antiphonary

Thanks to Robert I had come to detest Chigi and despise his companion profoundly. But how could I do useful research with that kind of prejudice? Impossible. In these circumstances I couldn't pursue my socio-historic research on Calvin and Geneva in 1536 and 1537, on the income of Chigi and Antonella, or Antonella's sexual behaviour.

I suddenly saw Robert in an ugly light: detestable, unbearable. I had the feeling that he was doing whatever he wanted with me, making me alternate between frustration and rage, now making me hate Antonella, now making me like her too much. Antonella was never a model of virtue, I'm quite aware of that; but after Robert's acerbic comments I took no more notice of that aspect of things (which according to my own hypothesis was quite flagrant in any case), and I even came to see her as a foolish victim of the aggressiveness of Chigi (a jealous man) and Robert (jealous of me, and above all ready to condemn a woman without proof, just for being a woman).

The hours, struck by the cathedral clock, passed solemnly and I couldn't sleep a wink. I wished that I could, like Antonella, sleep soundly (at least according to Chigi) but I could not. Antonella obsessed me (a murderess, if one can believe her defrocked companion, and a whore into the bargain if I believe Robert). In a man's world a free woman is easily accused of being a whore. She had no right to the benefit of the doubt — nor even a suspended sentence! It's a fact; man does not judge (as Péguy said), he condemns. It is so much easier, so much more convenient and reassuring! All the evil and filth are chalked up against women, without fail. And Robert, in this, was no different from other men. He was playing my prosecutor just as much as he was retroactively playing Antonella's ... How do I know that Chigi is objective and writes the truth? And what guarantee is there that Robert is different from the other men I've known, so far as women's behaviour is concerned?

The Antiphonary

There isn't any.

I now had proof that Robert was not the exception that supposedly confirms the rule. No, he was like Chigi and all the rest. And he probably thinks I'm a polished tart, a kind of little slut who took advantage of Jean-William and egged him on to murder a stranger (the druggist — but no, *that* he doesn't know about!).

And after all these horrors I suppose I was playing the sweet innocent with him, asking for his protection and offering him my pseudo-love! Oh, if that's the way Robert interprets what happened!

All I had to do — I mean during my insomnia — was recall the coarse allusions he had made about Antonella, and transpose or rather translate his aggressiveness against Antonella, and I was able to understand at once that Robert found my scientific interest in Antonella suspect, and that in my whole project he grasped only what related to Antonella, her pranks, her peccadillos, the prostitute side of her character, pre-judging from all this that I was myself emotionally involved in the erotic behaviour of this poor girl from Turin — whom I am more and more inclined to rehabilitate in my own mind, without informing him (Robert) that I am undertaking the process of her rehabilitation. Chigi, according to my new scheme of things, seems to me an absominable pimp who was capable of ignoring — or not deigning to admit — that he was living off the procurer's fees his dear Antonella brought home.

My eyes wide open, awake and furious, I felt the night hours pass slowly, gently, while Robert, fast asleep, rested from his work day and replenished, in deep sleep, all his depleted energy. My fury and bitterness had not receded. I was angry at Robert for speaking lightly of Antonella, and I felt that I would always resent him for this. He had ruined my thesis, ruined everything, by spitting, yes spitting, on people in whom I was interested.

The Antiphonary

I even developed a new opinion of Antonella, thus falling into the opposite error. I had no sense of proportion or measure, for I almost made a shameful cult of her ... In short, I would have done the same thing: *i.e.* sold myself willingly to strangers to get a little tangible profit — and of course come back at night, very late, with my stories of non-existent cabbage-barrows! A lie in a case like that is not too serious. That despicable spoiled priest (Chigi) was not worth much, and I (Christine Forestier) am inclined to think that he was afflicted with an impotence which was not only accidental (or temporary) but chronic. It was likely dull and devoid of surprise for Antonella when she slept every night in his bed. My God, if a woman isn't putting out for money, doesn't she have the right to do so just as a distraction from a sex life that is too boring, too colourless and discouraging? I say she does! And all that night while I was tossed about by my insomnia I blessed (retroactively and by transfer through time) Antonella Zimara for having done what she did if she did it! And tough tittie to Chigi, Robert and all the others like them!

When Robert awoke I was beside him looking at the robin's-egg-blue ceiling — its rough spots, its seas of tranquility, its little lunar craters.

Robert awoke very normally, without being too surprised to see me there impassive, silent, stiff as a corpse beside him. He didn't even take the trouble to say a word to me, but went at once to the bath. Nothing: an implacable silence, a kind of cold shower. I turned away in my bed like a poor idiot struggling with his conscience. I could not dismiss this kind of humiliation, I was petrified as I lay there by the senselessness of my defeat and, worse, of my regrets. And Robert, the winner, was shaving in there. Afterwards he came back into the room to dress, and calmly put on a suit with stripes of grey on grey — very elegant, by the way — and a blue shirt, as well as an Italian silk hankie to match his tie (dark red and scarlet). He took his time tying his Windsor knot and tipping it smartly, and the whole time cast not a single glance in my direction. I was saddened by his attitude, saddened because I did not approve of this obvious desire (Robert's) to freeze me out by paying me no attention. I had a (prophetic) feeling that he would regret it ... But that doesn't count. Perhaps he was right. I don't want to seem to imply that I knew then everything that happened later ... nor that I gave him the evil eye *(malocchio)*.

Robert finally left for his office without saying goodbye, without even eating his breakfast (bacon and eggs). He left without saying a word. And I stayed home, frightfully disappointed, desolate, unable to get over my feeling of failure.

The Antiphonary

That same day as I was having a short siesta on my bed the telephone rang twice. I picked it up. Nothing, nobody there. I said "Hello!" several times. My answer was the most implacable silence. I didn't think for a moment that it meant anything. I thought it was simply one of those accidents that happen every day in a bilingual city where children, moreover, are allowed to use the phone.

I dropped off to sleep again. A few minutes later the telephone rang again. The same odd situation; disquieting. There was nobody on the other end of the line, or rather there was someone who said nothing, which is even more terrifying. This time I was really upset.

Right away I picked up the phone again and dialed Robert's office. He was out for the moment. He must, I thought, have gone for lunch with a client or a colleague. A late lunch at that. I asked his secretary to have him call me back as soon as he came in.

In fact Robert phoned me a few minutes later. He had just come back from lunching with a director of the GFC (General Finance Company) and he told me that this director (Lacour by name) had offered him a very important job, highly paid, as a director with Sorel Industries, which is state-controlled. And he asked me right away if I were all right, if I were well. I said I was perhaps a little sad, but I was sure he would know how to cheer me up. It all depended on him.

Robert said, very quietly in the phone, that he loved me more than anything in the world, and he asked me to forgive him for the way he had been that morning. I said at once that he had my love and my forgiveness and anything else he wanted. But wouldn't his new job with Sorel Industries mean leaving Montreal for Sorel? He said no; the head office was located at 186 St. James St. West. Robert came back to the attack and asked me if I liked the idea of his working for GFC. I said I did. I was sure I would be happy if he were and, of course, if it brought a little more money ...

"Then," said Robert, "if you want to please me, you'll start practising medicine again."

"Are you sure?" I asked.

"Yes, my love. I beg you to do it. Would you like to take up your profession again? Tell me."

"Oh, Robert, you know ... If you ask me to do it, I will, and gladly. But you must really swear that it wouldn't trouble you in any way!"

"Christine," he said, "I swear it. Yes, I swear it."

Later that afternoon (it must have been about 5) I heard a door close. It was Robert, home early from the office. I was just in the kitchen chopping vegetables for our meal. I wiped my hands hastily to go and meet Robert. I could imagine him on the landing, in his dark blue raincoat. Then there was the sound of the street door closing a second time. Robert opened the apartment door and stood smiling at me. Then he half-turned, horrified. I understood, but too late. He had been hit by two bullets at close range. He fell down unconscious, wounded in the forehead and the ear.

I took a step or two toward him. Then I saw Jean-William at the bottom of the stairs coolly tucking away his gun (I recognized the pistol from San Diego). I was terrified for my own safety; but Jean-William made no move. He merely said cynically:

"O.K., beautiful. All you have to do is give my name to

the police. So long!''

I feared the worst, that Robert was dead. But my old doctor's reflex gave me hope against all hope that he could be saved. He was wounded in the forehead and just below the right ear. What I had to do was call the Montreal Police or a hospital. Jean-William, highly pleased with himself, went out the front door (after delivering his lapidary little speech) and I immediately phoned the Montreal Police. Two minutes later a patrol-car ambulance from Station 14 stopped at the door. The two officers got out fast, revolvers drawn, and joined me on the first floor up (where we lived).

''You have to hurry,'' I said to the first. ''He's bleeding and unconscious.''

''Cause?'' said the second.

''Attempted murder.''

The two policemen ambulance-drivers busied themselves with Robert's body, tying it and, with some trouble, getting it onto a stretcher which they swiftly carried down and lifted delicately into their ambulance (a blue-white station wagon, number 14-6). One of the policemen told me to get in the back beside Robert's stretcher. Then they took off at high speed, all sirens wailing, for the north, toward Saint-Justine (as I first thought), then after a few zig-zags toward the Sacré-Coeur Hospital. I knew it from having done a few stints there as a student, no more. The police car stopped in front of the emergency entrance, and the two policemen brought the stretcher quickly inside. I followed them and was joined by one of the policemen, who excused himself for bringing the patient so far (it was because of radioed instructions received in the meantime). He asked me to follow him into a small side room where he asked me a few questions for his report. Pure routine, he said. Name of the wounded man. Who should be notified. Relationship to the victim. Identity of the attacker. (I couldn't make up my mind to say openly that his name was Jean-William Forestier and that I was his lawful wife.) Details about myself. Etc. I really didn't find the questioning too bad (it was quite tactfully done, by the way). I thanked the officer sincerely for having done his duty so quickly and well.

After these formalities he asked to be excused for having bothered me at such a time, and wished me good luck. I stayed there, silent, worried, upset, almost traumatized. From what I knew of surgery it would be a difficult and delicate business extracting the bullets, and a long and arduous recovery would follow.

Above all I feared that Robert might have been shot in the lung or in the reticular area, and that a serious lesion was inevitable, fatally so. But obviously I wouldn't find out anything until surgery had been performed. So I waited, simply waited. "Simply!" What an inadequate word! Nothing would be simple from now on.

I thought of Jean-William, but ineffectually, without the slightest logic in my ideas, without basing my speculations on even the flimsiest reality. I could still see him after he had fired his two shots at Robert, insolent, standing there, saying: "O.K., all you have to do is give my name to the police now," or something of the sort. But it was horribly true! Since that moment I had no more reported him to the police than I had in San Diego (about the druggist). God knows I didn't want to be considered his accomplice! But I was behaving like one. I had made no report in San Diego, none in Montreal (where the frightful episode had just taken place in the course of which Jean-William had shot Robert down brutally, with no subtlety, without the least consideration or reflection). Jean-William had gone mad — beyond a doubt — in San Diego. And he had gone mad again in Montreal (showing that the few days between his first signs of trouble and the brutal murder of Robert had not changed him for the better).

And here was I refusing to turn him in, stupefied as I was by so much horror and violence, though I had every reason to denounce him. Here I was, not saying his name, not mentioning him to the Montreal police. Inexcusable! My behaviour was inexplicable! What did I have to lose or fear? Reprisals? Good God, did Jean-William have to attack me personally and try to kill me in order to incite me to accuse and officially denounce him??? Was it some vestige of conjugal love that had held me back? But that was madness, quite unjustifiable. I should go ahead with my denunciation just to prevent him from doing further harm — before he killed me too!!! The hours went by. Robert was still in the operating room, undergoing multiple operations of a surgical and neurological nature whose sole purpose was to bring him back to life. And all the time I paced the waiting room of the emergency ward of Sacré-Coeur, conscious of my guilt and of my hideous complicity with a man I detested intensely and pitilessly. I was ashamed of myself.

The Antiphonary

Chigi had found work (not badly paid) at the Gryphe printing shop in Geneva. He was no longer dependent on the (somewhat suspect) income of his companion Antonella. More and more he had acquired the habit (common among the overseers and proof-readers working with him) of leaving home early in the morning and returning around dusk. Antonella has usually left for work at the Market, for she had insisted on continuing. Chigi thus had to make his own meal, after which he sat down at the table by the window where he had the best light for writing or re-writing Jules-César Beausang's text.

The young defrocked priest, accustomed to the solitude of his Turin presbytery, had easily grown used to being alone in his Geneva apartment. When Antonella came home he was already sound asleep. And he rose at dawn like the other workers. He felt pleasantly free in this life, for he no longer depended on what Antonella earned. Obviously he was victim of a certain disenchantment: he had not thought that his life with Antonella would be this sinister desert, without affection or voluptuousness. But when he saw the fate of his fellow-workers, his own seemed neither more nor less bearable than theirs. These people (the workers in Gryphe's printing establishment) had no specific kinds of happiness. When they went home their day was already ended (or almost). When they spoke of their wives it was either to complain, or to rejoice (matter of age?) at the festivities planned for Saturday evening or Sunday. This was true for Chigi as well, resigned like his companions to the dull existence of an ordinary workman. If anything in his life was different from theirs it was, indeed, that Antonella worked Saturday and Sunday too, so that one way or the other he never managed to have a complete night with her. This involuntary continence enabled him, in fact, to accomplish something each day in writing or modifying the (so-called) diary of Jules-César Beausang. But Chigi's companions found his wife's hours both unacceptable and implausible. They told him repeatedly what they thought on the subject. Apparently Chigi was being made a fool of right and left. He should be a little more suspicious of his ''wife's'' overtime.

One evening, just before sundown (when Mont Blanc was turning black, as the good people of Geneva say), Leonico Chigi came home early from the printer's. He had decided to throw up everything — his work, his salary, his security, Antonella, and Geneva. He had become strangely detached. He left his place of work in the middle of the afternoon (without asking permission) and walked along the waterfront to his apartment. For some months now he had not come home from work so early. He felt as if he were on holiday. His thoughts flew round in his head as free as birds. He thought of Beausang, his stay in Basel, his voyage to Chivasso, his sad end. Poor Beausang, said Chigi to himself, he ran away from Ghent because his wife was unfaithful to him (at least that was what he had written and alleged) — poor Beausang. His existence seemed to have been the very opposite of the life he should have had. He had had nothing but misfortunes, mischances, rebuffs and disappointments. And he had not even God to console his sadness, for God was absent from Jules-César Beausang's life. At least this was a conclusion one could clearly draw from his various works. Beausang — like many of his contemporaries — was a nonbeliever inclined to the most radical agnosticism (despite his profession of faith as a Gomarist). We could doubtless explain such a masked abjuration of all religious confessions by his despair over his own existence.

Thus Chigi reflected on the first author of the manuscript which he, Chigi, was in the process of re-making and re-composing. The more progress he made in his project the more he grew determined to interweave his own intimate diary (since his departure from Turin) with the text of the famous doctor from Ghent. At the same time he was hatching the idea of producing an entirely apocryphal tale in which Chigi would tell his own story, interweaving a fictitious (imagined) life of Jules-César Beausang. And so on and so on ... His mind was bubbling with an endless succession of thoughts, and a kind of intoxicating elation came over him, he had no idea why. Perhaps, he said to himself, because I am a free man and because my head is bursting with the power of new ideas, because I left the printing shop early today and in a moment I will see my Antonella. She will most certainly be surprised; but at last I will be able to tell her all my ideas, my new vision of things, and I will kiss her ... kiss her ... Something told him that this day in his life was not like other days. He felt endowed with a freedom such as he had never known.

(And I, telling you this, I know what I'm talking about. I won't beat around the bush. It is time for Chigi, wandering through these written lines and along the waterfront of Geneva, to arrive at last at the rooms he occupies with his companion Antonella. The delaying action is there not because I want to play games with the reader who — some day — will hold my book in his hand, but because, my life having turned the way it has, I find that beyond the slightest doubt I have a tendency to emphasize those aspects of reality which echo my own, and to dwell especially on all that is laden with horror and surprise. Dr A. Franconi has just offered me the use of his office, and I'm writing on prescription pads that I found in one of his drawers. In fact, I have time to kill. For the last 4 days, during which

The Antiphonary

I have not left the hospital, Robert has not been able to say a coherent word to me. He did not die from Jean-William's bullets; but his wound, in the lower junction of the rhinencephalic allocortex, damaged the limbic (or practognosic) system — which means that he will suffer for some time from fairly severe language disturbances. Dr Franconi told me yesterday that Robert had experienced an uncinate crisis (Hill), as well as ocular troubles, *i.e.* nystagmus, and lateral homonomous hemianopsia with some hallucinating in the dark hemicampus. These problems of equilibration in the optical field are apparently very serious. Dr Franconi seems most responsible and competent, especially in neurology. When I finished my medical studies I had acquired no more than a few rudimentary ideas in that area. And I suppose that even those are now out of date. The "Uncinate fit" for example was completely unknown to me. But let us go back to Chigi, for I feel almost certain that I will never publish my thesis on 16th century medicine. If I continued I would have an opportunity to deal with Jules-César Beausang. Since I shall never finish the thesis I simply scribble away about Beausang and Chigi. And so we find our dear spoiled priest striding toward his lodgings . . .)

He stepped along more briskly as he drew near his own neighbourhood, greeting the shopkeepers he knew. Then, once in the entrance of his building, he rushed inside and pushed open the door without a sound (no doubt so that Antonella would be the more agreeably surprised). Antonella was not in the kitchen which the couple used as living room. Chigi closed the outside door and tiptoed toward their bedchamber. When he opened the door he saw their room plunged in complete darkness. Before his eyes could grow accustomed to the change he heard the voice of a stranger, then Antonella's, murmuring. What he finally saw was a horror to him: Antonella, naked, on the bed, submitting to the immodest caresses of a man (obviously drunk) who was also naked and lying on the bed. Following a strange reflex, Chigi closed the door of the bedroom again (which no doubt brought the other two partly to their senses) and calmly, or so he says, opened drawers one after the other to prepare a bundle of necessities — bread, cheese, a few utensils. Then (at least so he tells it) he saw the breadknife in the bottom of a drawer. He grasped it firmly, while the two on the other side of the wall continued their debauch. He declares that his previous entry had not disturbed them. This may be partially true, a detail that underlines the abomination of the scene. Antonella was doubtless dead drunk and her companion little better. Chigi opened the door again. Knife in hand, he rushed at the bed and sank the knife into the fresh and sweating body of Antonella (who uttered her death-cry). Then Chigi sought (with a certain hesitancy) for the other, whom he intended to deal with in the same way. To his great surprise he received a kick directly in his middle. He was stunned for a moment (he probably fell to the floor). Antonella was breathing her last on the bed, close by him, but he noticed nothing. Chigi opened his eyes just in time to see the stranger (a man of considerable size) dressing hastily and making his escape. Chigi was suffering horribly from the blow he had received in the belly. He thought he was seriously hurt. But something told him he must not tarry there doing nothing. Strangely enough, he watched through half-closed eyes as the stranger took to his heels unpunished. Then, without a glance at Antonella's corpse, Chigi swiftly collected some clothing, took the manuscript and some cash that he had kept hidden in the base of a lamp, and fled without further ado across the neighbours' roofs and down the stairway of another building to the street. Already a crowd was screaming, shouting, doubtless passing along the story of what had happened in the lodging of those "dirty Italians." Chigi took a back street and walked quietly until sundown. When he stopped he was already near the border

The Antiphonary

of Geneva, in Céligny. He spent the night at an inn where, before going to sleep, he set down these events, omitting neither his crime nor his shameful sin. Never mind, he said to himself, I am going to make a new life for myself in the Kingdom of France. Next day, Chigi succeeded in crossing the French border near Divonne (using shepherds' paths and field roads so as to avoid whatever police might be underway). Once in France he stopped at the presbytery of St-Germain, in Bellegarde (a nearby town situated past the westernmost point of Geneva). He asked the priest on duty for a private interview. Once in the presbytery he revealed himself as the abbot Leonico Zimara of Turin, and told how he had been obliged in Switzerland to disguise himself in order to pass through those Protestant cantons, where he had had his bad moments. At once the French priest, happy to be of service to a Piedmontese colleague in trouble, offered him food and lodging for as long as he wished to stay. Only too pleased, the abbot Zimara moved into a little attic room reserved for visiting priests. At supper he met the curé and other priests of the parish. He won their good opinion by showing off his scientific knowledge and expressing certain notions on the lack of piety among the common folk. Suddenly one of the French priests asked him a series of questions on the subject of the infiltration of the church by various heresies. It was a kind of test, but the former priest from Turin (Zimara now) came through with high marks. He knew enough about the heresies to show that he could refute them, but also that he was beyond question on the proper side. The parish priest, so Chigi reports, said that nowadays there were all sorts of people wandering the countryside and inculcating these heresies among the peasants and the whole population. ''We have the same thing in Piedmont,'' replied the unfrocked abbot from Turin. He went on with a peroration whose self-assurance aroused his colleagues' enthusiasm (and perhaps dissipated their suspicions and doubts about this intruder passing for a priest). One thing is certain: the day was won by our Chigi (alias Beausang, alias the killer from Geneva). The rest ...

The Antiphonary

No, I shall never publish my thesis. I'm sure of that. So I might as well tell things one at a time. How I found out about Jean-William's return trip by car after San Diego and all the rest of it. His return was described to me indirectly by Robert, who in turn had found out from his wife Suzanne who had had a phone-call from Jean-William from Phoenix (Arizona). Jean-William, hyped-up on alcohol or some kind of medicine, had suddenly thought it would be very clever to phone Suzanne long-distance to tell her what she could expect as soon as I came back from San Diego, which wouldn't be long. He told Suzanne I was going to steal her husband; that I'd already done it many times (to his "certain knowledge" he said, according to Robert). And he told her all kinds of horrors about me — horrors (fortunately) that Robert would likely be telling her shortly. Suzanne wasn't as shocked as Jean-William would have liked. She told Robert when he came home that she had had this strange and slightly mad phone call. Robert reacted coolly, but pointed out to his wife that if Jean-William came on the line again with his weird calls she had only to hang up in his ear, provided, of course, she was certain she recognized the voice. For, as Robert said, one had to watch out for imposters and maniacs. That settled that. In fact, Robert was less upset by the incident itself than by Suzanne, who was so quiet about it. At that moment I must have been in San Modesto, flopped in front of the TV, dressing my wounds. But next day Suzanne (still in Montreal) had another phone-call from Jean-William, this time from Denver

The Antiphonary

(Colorado); and that night, instead of telling Robert about it, she kept it to herself, for she was already shaken by the accusations of infidelity made against her husband Robert and myself. (At least that was Suzanne's version to Robert at the time of their separation). So that there was more of the same kind of blabbing about the whole business, by long distance, with Jean-William (sizing up the whole situation and doubtless foreseeing my return) venting by phone all the fury of his accusatory delirium. One might say that thanks to the incessant calls made by Jean-William to Suzanne I was made aware — as soon as I saw Robert again — of all sorts of plausible details about the route taken by Jean-William, and of the fact that the very day before he reached home he was still in Buffalo (or 800 miles from Montreal), which meant that I probably had a margin of two or three hours to go to the St. Lambert apartment to pick up a few possessions and clothes.

Poor Suzanne! She had to take it on the chin, hearing by phone all those horrors invented by Jean-William's sick mind. Of course, the monstrous details about himself were given a paranoid twist: Jean-William warned Suzanne that I would certainly tell her — through Robert — that Jean-William had tried to kill me (and perhaps that he had even tried to murder god-knows-who — never mentioning the druggist, of course, for he didn't know I had witnessed the killing that day, close by the scene of the crime). Most upsetting of all (I mean for Suzanne) were Jean-William's sobbing fits. He would stay for minutes on the line crying like a child. Suzanne would try to quiet him, reason with him, make him tell everything so as to get it out of his system. Nothing doing. Jean-William would go on sobbing indefinitely. Suzanne was upset (she was thinking of the long-distance charges he would have to pay, there on the spot) but most of all she was sorry for him. She had known Jean-William as quite a jolly person. She knew (I had told her the secret)

143

that Jean-William suffered from epilepsy. But she could never have believed that he could go to pieces this way or behave so distressingly. In fact, she lost her grip in the face of this invading, obsessive reality with which Jean-William bombarded her by phone. She was flooded by it, swept off her feet. It was all too powerful and impressive! She began to think that some of Jean-William's stories were based on fact, and that out of all this flood of words a certain number revealed horrible truths, which Jean-William, at the height of his delirium, rightly felt as injuries to his self-respect! Of course, I always assumed that Robert, when he brought me up to date on all this, tactfully left out certain details that Suzanne must have retailed to him with glee. He spared me the word-for-word accounts of her exchanges with him. And we never after spoke about Jean-William (except perhaps once or twice, evasively — for I was always terrified that some detail would set him off on the subject of my past), nor about Suzanne. But when I was alone in the apartment the thought of Jean-William occasionally crossed my mind, and I would shudder. I was afraid he would try to find me in Montreal and murder me, point blank, on sight. Sometimes, before going to sleep in Robert's arms (he always went to sleep before me), I would suddenly imagine I had left the front door open or neglected the chain. Then I'd get up — without waking Robert — and go out on tiptoe to see if all was well. These fears attacked me often and at the oddest times, for example, in the midst of a meal (when Robert and I were sitting at dinner) or in the evening, when we were watching TV. But no doubt my fear instilled in me an obstinate silence about Jean-William. I never, or hardly ever, mentioned his name in front of Robert. It was a kind of taboo — vague, I admit, but obsessive and tenacious. Maybe I should have spoken to Robert. But he would only have been needlessly upset. Unless he was getting phone calls from Jean-William in his office, and not telling me ...

The Antiphonary

Threats, perhaps, threats to my life, announcements (by Jean-William) that he would kill me, sooner or later, when he decided to — or that he'd kill us both (Robert and me) in bed together. But (two minutes sleep, then a start, wakened by noise in the next apartment, nurses laughing . . .) if Robert has been getting such calls he'll tell me himself, for he will surely tell me everything when he regains his consciousness and power of speech. For the moment it still seems a good idea not to go back to our apartment, so I'll accept Dr Franconi's invitation to sleep here on a cramped little hospital cot set up in his office.

It's not all that comfortable, to be sure, and there's always noise. But I manage to catch a half-hour's sleep here and there. And any moment now I'm going to lie down (after a little wash) and try to sleep for a few hours. I feel heavy with fatigue, worn out, incapable, in fact, of going on with this book in a sensible way, for its form is gradually disintegrating and tends more and more to escape my intentions. The multitude of words hang together in a powdery screen: suddenly I can see nothing, I am blinded by the oblique refractions of solar light. Everything is luminous in this nebula that surrounds me, and yet I know very well that everything is dull, there is nothing shining here! It's high time I lay down on this clinic bed and gave myself up to sleep for a few hours.

The Antiphonary

Dead of night. The hospital is humming with continual noises of every kind. You'd really think everything was done to surround hospitalized patients with the worst possible sonorous ambiance. Or that no place could be noisier than one set apart for curing the sick, and that noise was the best thing in the world to effect that cure. I would never have believed it. My years in medicine (and the periods spent in hospitals) never taught me as much. Yet the short stay I am making now (because of Robert's hospitalization) has revealed to me this particularly irritating truth. But never mind . . .

I went back to sleep later. I must have slept for a few hours (two or three) for I feel quite recovered from my fatigue.

The Antiphonary

Robert is still in coma. He is now being fed intravenously (two or three tubes at once). If all goes well he will regain consciousness in a few hours, according to Dr Franconi. Every time I go near Robert I have the strange feeling that he is about to speak to me. This feeling is upsetting and gives me an acute sensation of privation, solitude and abandonment.

I can hardly wait to speak to him, and also to exchange certain confidences with him. But above all I want to leave this hospital with him in a private ambulance and take him home again. Should I inform his ex-wife, Suzanne, of what has happened? ... It would only upset her needlessly, and she might even find it cruel of me to remind her of Robert just when he is in a critical state in hospital ... And, indeed, she might be right. It may be better, just out of politeness, if I don't speak about it to her. For Suzanne — and I admit it freely — has never done me any harm.

The Antiphonary

After a few days in Bellegarde the priest from Turin (Chigi-Zimara) set out for Bourg-en-Bresse, where he arrived fitted out in a soutane given to him on his departure by his colleagues in Bellegarde. He had also been presented with a bundle of notes valid in the Kingdom of France, with the help of which he counted on reaching Lyon, the town of bookseller-publishers. The road to Bourg-en-Bresse he found charming. He went through several small villages such as Ambérieu, and passed between wide, fertile fields, all cultivated and covered with vegetation that promised a healthy harvest. The closer he came to Bourg the more numerous the farmhouses became. Most reassuring . . .

In Bourg-en-Bresse, a smaller city than Turin (and less civilized, he thought) the abbot slept in the presbytery of the parish of Saint-Jean-de-Dieu, in the very middle of town. The curé and the priests (the others were vicars) appeared most hospitable; and above all, less suspicious than the priests of Bellegarde, who were conditioned by their proximity to Geneva to be over-cautious about anything that might smell of the neighbouring heresy of Calvinism. Bourg-en-Bresse was completely different from the border town of Bellegarde. It was a kind of small capital of a prosperous farming region and rich in wines of all sorts (the vineyards of the Jura and the foothills of the French Jura produced white wines that were much appreciated). This was quite a change from Geneva, a city hostile and Calvinist in the worst sense of the word (if the word can indeed be used as an insult), a city that stank of hypocrisy, contentiousness, frigidity and xenophobia (he had only to be called a "dirty Italian" a few times to become aware of the latter). Geneva — the city where his defunct companion, Antonella, had indulged in a shameful commerce with passing travellers, with idiots from the poorer class or Protestants who needed to unbutton their principles. A filthy city, Geneva, the proud, pretentious bastion of Calvinism and the heresy of reform.

He had money enough to continue to Lyon without making too many sacrifices and without resorting to begging. That was reassuring. Moreover the priests of Bourg-en-Bresse had boasted about how safe the road was between Bourg and Lyon, as well as about the beauty of the Rhone, which makes a loop in Lyon before going on down through its luminous valley toward the Mediterranean. Lyon, for the priests in Bourg, was the big city, the exciting capital, the *nec plus ultra* of civilization and urbanization. In short, Chigi was itching to start when he heard such praises of the great city of the Rhone. He set off on foot one fine summer day near the beginning of June. By noon, when the peasants were resting in the fields, Chigi began to feel the effects of that gentle heat of the Midi, which augured well for the climate of the city he was approaching. He rested at the foot of a great tree, in the shade, so as not to fall from weariness as he walked. And when darkness came he arrived in a village, where he decided to pass the night. For it was by no means recommended to stroll after dark on the highways of the Kingdom. Everyone deplored this state of affairs, and no one yet had been able to explain it satisfactorily.

But while he is resting God-knows-where between Bourg-en-Bresse and Lyon, I, Christine, am wondering what to make of the contradictory information I'm getting about Robert's health. At times I'm led to think he's improving; at others, I'm less reassured. And now they're talking about a second operation to protect the hypothalamus against some threatened infection. That means — and I know this from experience — that Robert is suffering from thalamic hyperpathia (Krupners' syndrome). My God! So it's serious, really serious! The little I know only aggravates my anxiety. Suddenly I start thinking about thalamic cenestopathia and degenerative lateral lesions (described by Stern and Gunthal). I can't bear now to speak to the nurses or any of Dr Franconi's many assistants, some of whom have gone so far as to mention (among themselves, but I overheard) the word hemidecortication (which would mean that Robert, if operated on in this way, would be deprived of various nociceptive responses and would remain seriously handicapped).

Now I must rest a little. Yes, I will rest a little, sleep, and get back my strength if I still can ... at least until I can talk all this over with Dr Franconi.

The Antiphonary

There was a strange sunrise over Montreal today. Mysterious spectral lights probed the sky over Cartierville and the north shore of Rivière des Prairies near Laval. It all seemed marvellously majestic to me, as I leaned on the little window that is my porthole, watching the disappearance of the absolute black of the night before. There is no doubt that I have become abnormally sensitive since I have taken up cohabitation, in Sacré-Coeur Hospital, with Robert, the man of my life — gravely wounded by the man who formerly considered me the woman of his life! This sinister house where they think nothing of trepanning a man (with concurrent and often inherent lesions) seems to me, this shining morning in June, like an asylum designed to precipitate mental alienation and morbidity, no less! I think the proximity of so many gasping bodies and opened skulls (or bleeding brains!) has made me purely and simply mad; or very close to it — neurotic, sick, unable to experience reality other than in disgust and nausea. In fact, time is passing. Robert stirs in the depth of his coma, and nothing changes. I would like to fly away, for I feel totally imprisoned here. But I know quite well that Jean-William (that adorable, unpunished killer) is waiting for me around the corner with a pistol as big as his great shameless, erected penis . . .   Oh, I'm ashamed! These words that I'm trying to put in line on Dr Franconi's prescription pad seem horrible to me. I don't want to die with this impression of vomit and disgust. I must get hold of myself. But it's true, I should run away from this hospital where Robert is being chopped into sausage under elegant headings like hemidecortication and other pieces of surgical madness. I should run out, risk death. Never look back, leave the man I love to every kind of exteroceptive degeneration of the body surface and all the discomforts of cortical arrhythmia, as well as the discrete after-effects of multiple choreo-athetoid hemiplegias and the more or less precipitate strychnisation of his whole organism!

But there it is, I'm still here, struck by affective paralysis. Nothing stirs inside me any more. I am preserved with all the coquetry of an authenticated mummy. I have no appetite, feel no thirst, no physical desire to bring me back to normal. Even sexual desire (in me) has been remarkably suppressed. I am dear nothing Christine, the little prude, the spoiled little brat that gets herself raped in San Diego by a would-be Spanish buccaneer. I think I've lost them, my poor marbles, and quite a while ago. It's obvious! I'm bursting with proof of it! I'm a kind of living mire, a pile of corruption that merely extends itself (through what aberrant mechanism?) along these bi-dimensional pages taken from the desk of the man who will slice in equal thicknesses the brain of my own love ... Aaaaaaaah!

The Antiphonary

Chigi arrived in Lyon. He went at once to the city centre, rue de la Poste (where the bookseller-publishers had their offices). In a single hour toward the end of one afternoon he managed to find work. And the next day, in conversation with Guillaume Vascosan (his employer), he had already sold the manuscript by Jules-César Beausang, as well as a projected biography of our dear friend Beausang, for he was one of a very few to know how the Doctor's life had ended. What made perhaps the greatest impressin on Vascosan was the amount of fragmentary material Chigi had in his possession, which might constitute a second book. A good stroke of business.

What I haven't yet said is that Chigi's doings interest me less and less. Let him play the hoity-toity newly-rich over Jules-César Beausang's bones, pretending for the benefit of Vascosan to revere his memory in a very concrete way: so far as I'm concerned his behaviour is a sad and empty story. And anyway I have other things to worry about than what that abbot from Turin is up to. For one, I ended the previous chapter of this book on a note that was particularly frustrating (to the reader): and rightly so! I neglected at that point to tell the truth. When I was just getting out of Dr Franconi's bed, Dr Franconi in person made an appearance in his office. He made as if to go out again at once, for I was rather sketchily attired, naked in fact, and emerging from between the sheets. I reflected, then at once I spoke to the dear Doctor.

"Don't worry, Doctor, please! I'll only be a second getting

something on. I'm the one who should be saying excuse me. After all, it's your office, isn't it!''

All I needed to do was hold my tongue. But I didn't. And that was the (superfluous) triggering factor. Dr Franconi hesitated an instant in the doorway, then (because it opened onto the corridor) he hastily closed it for my privacy, for I had begun to dress.

Oh, God, what words can I use to describe what followed? My courage fails me. And I have the embarrassing feeling that the reader has already guessed I am about to relate something horrible and revolting. At least that is what I imagine, and who is to tell me I'm wrong? ... I'm right, beyond a doubt: and therefore it's best — in all simplicity — to overcome the shame I feel and tell things just as they happened. Well ... I was just getting dressed (after getting out of bed, in that office ... you see ...) when the Doctor came up from behind and, putting his arms around me, threw me back on the bed. (I should perhaps add that I was more than half aware of his approach: I even found it peculiarly indecent of me to take my time as I did, while he was there two steps away from me ...) The rest is rather sordid. Must I indeed tell everything, describe in detail the Doctor's caresses and his unchaste initiatives, as well as the surprise I simulated in order (I suppose) to attenuate the monstrousness of what happened in the short time that elapsed following upon my emergence from the bed and leading up to our mutual orgasm? It was certainly not the moment for such an experience, it was inconceivable, and yet ...

"Aha, little lady, you're keeping big secrets from your husband's doctor!''

"What secrets?'' I asked. (But I knew more or less what he was getting at.)

"This tummy of yours, eh?''

"What do you mean? I don't know what you're referring to,

154

The Antiphonary

Doctor. And what on earth do you want from me?'' (I knew very well that he was swiftly undoing his pants and his doctor's smock . . .)

"What? You don't know what I mean? Strange . . . And yet there's no mistake . . ."

(His caresses began to thrust and penetrate, they became an irreversible invasion — for me at least. And I ceded hypocritically to his advances.)

"Good heavens, Doctor, what do you mean?"

"Oh, nothing, just that you've got a pretty little tummy, all rounded out like a birdcage.''

"My stomach???? What do you mean? I don't understand!''

"How many months?''

(His caresses left me soft and helpless. I had no resistance to such hyper-acute titillation.)

"Ohhhhhh . . .''

"What?'' he said, "Is that nice?''

"No, I don't know what you . . . No, stop, please stop, I'm not this kind of woman, you're wrong about me, Doctor . . .''

"I'm not caressing you, it's this child you carry so splendidly. Believe me, this is merely . . .''

(He was already inside me, all movement, fluidity, warmth . . . How could I cheat like this?)

"Don't worry,'' he told me, "I double-locked the door. Nobody can hear us, no one will ever know. I am no more than an episode in your life, you will never see me again. But I find you lovely, lovely in your pregnancy! Your belly is already swollen, your breasts are expanding . . . I tell you I love you, and please don't think I'm trying to take advantage of your situation.''

(I was about to open like a flower and die of pleasure in his arms. I turned to see him, look at him, kiss his mouth,

155

for he had held me from behind from the start, and I felt that
our poor embrace was about to end!)

"No, no, please no!" (But I was already crying out, my voice
was completely distorted, beyond its register, I was almost
screaming . . .)

"Don't tell me, now, that you don't like it."

(He was pernicious, but I was monstrous, frightful, vile . . .
Aaaaah, but I had a nameless feeling that my belly was gently
dissolving under me, that I would disintegrate under the coming
shock of pleasure . . . What I didn't know was that this doctor
was going to reach his peak at almost the same time as myself!
Never — no really, never had it been so intense, so hallucinatory!
There could be no looking back, we had already gone too far.
We could never deny this dazzling beginning, never check the
diffusive explosion that would leave us in cinders forever . . .)

"No, no, no . . ." (These were my last articulated words,
my last gestures of resistance, my last impulses of false modesty,
serving at the same time as a paradoxical prelude to a shivering,
unforgettable, perfect paroxysm of pleasure . . .)

Afterwards, the most incredible disappointment. Nothing is
more upsetting than the collapse of muscular tonicity following
a too-intense gratification. I rose to my feet. Then, this companion
of mine (who had turned out to be magnificent) simply adjusted
his clothing as if nothing had happened, and mopped his brow
(for it was covered with sweat). Could it be? Was my life turned
to horror? Or was horror my due, must I wallow in it, feed
upon it? I had the hateful sensation of stumbling, falling, I was
a wretch again, nothing but a wife with child by one stranger
and capable of copulating with yet another stranger while my
husband, nearby was to undergo "intensive reanimation treatment" — and that in about one quarter of an hour! Oh, truly,
I would never be able to tell this episode to Robert! If it had
to be, let him die in his bed in this hospital, and never, never,

The Antiphonary

never hear a word of what I had done. And let me never survive those painful moments that followed: the stop, the brutal cutoff of pleasure; at first, blind ecstasy, and then - the details of getting dressed, mutual embarrassment, long silences during which my shining companion was obliged to comb his hair and wash his face and neck, while I fastened my stockings to my garter-belt and put on my dress.

The Antiphonary

"Every author," says Jules-César Beausang, "adds something to the object of his discourse." And elsewhere, "The story means nothing, and yet has meaning." God, let me be an author, so that I may add something to the object of my discourse! For I know only too well that my story means little, means nothing whatsoever! And yet, it is not just a story. I should say, alas, that it is no story but the strict and abominable truth. The true masterpiece (*opus consummatum*) is that which transposes into a perfect form all the profundity of the "quadrivial sciences." At least that was the opinion of Jules-César Beausang, according to the theories of allegory current in his time. But how far am I from allegory when I sink to the abomination of desolation, into nothingness! Oh, how far from any masterpiece or any kind or variant of allegory! Here is no *opus consummatum* but a collection of poor enigmas not worth solving, full of factitious depths (*trobar clus*)!

I slip into an *ornata facilitas* (*"nimis duris et ampullosis translationibus,"* as Geffroi de Vinsauf would have put it). Yet the *ornata facilitas* is not the bottom of the scale, if one thinks of the *stilorum incongrua variatio* or the *vitia colletaria* as described by Jean de Garlande. No, I have not yet lost my hold in this dark and briny sea *(stilo humili . . .)* on which I am in the process of precipitating a shipwreck vitiated by a mishmash of styles. As Jules-César Beausang put it so well, incoherence engenders obscurity. We probably have here one of the maxims of the theoreticians of "flowery and even affected elegance"

158

The Antiphonary

— G. de Vinsauf (an Englishman), Alain de Lille (a man of the world), or Gervais de Melkley (a miserable failure reduced to the tautologies of his *cantilenae*). Of all these dictamenic treatises the most widely known is beyond question that by Richard of Thetford, along with that of Robert of Basevorn. (In any case Jules-César Beausang read and followed the practice of these two authors as a matter of preference.) As for me, dear readers, I prefer — and this must be obvious — a Thomas Waleys or a Fortunatian: you have my *prothema*, openly exposed (in the Waleys manner), unfolding, afterwards, into a theme and a repetition of the theme *(introductio)*, after which the *partitio* is developed on several points (see above); then I confirm, perorate, present my *argumentum*, declare and distinguish, and establish the correlations between the diverse portions of my discourse. As Robert of Basevorn so well expressed it: *"Inter omnes curiositates istam reputo simpliciter majorem et difficiliorem, et ideo pauci apti sunt ea uti prout opertet"* (*Summa de Arte Praedicatoria*, by Robert de Basevorn, p. 68, Ed. Béroé, 1674, Basel). You may object that I run rather to the *jocatio opportuna*, so dear to Basevorn! And that I smear it on by the tubeful . . . And in my exhausted state I will not even try to refute what you say. In fact — giving in to the *jocatio opportuna* style — I make what use I can of horrors *(falsis verborum)*, such as those committed in the office of this doctor in the Sacré-Coeur hospital one morning at around 7:00 a.m. Nothing allegorical about that pitiful episode, which exudes — alas! — a trivial verity and an overdose of nauseating reality. There is nothing here, believe me, which can establish any relationship between my wretched literary undertaking and that of Sidonius Apollinaris or Guillaume de Conches, no, nothing that is comparable with the project of euphemistic falsification of a Leonico Chigi or a Godefroid de Saint-Victor or a Milon de Bec . . .

The Antiphonary

If this is becoming irritating (to read, I mean) you should drop me here, for — on this you can rely — you have not suffered your last disappointment. The incident (if I can use the word) of Dr Franconi must have revealed a repulsive side of me in no way corresponding to the "exemplar" extolled by Alain de Lille. On the contrary, I feel that with this episode I have scuttled myself in the eyes of any possible reader who might until then have put up with my hisperic turgidity, my psychomachic capework, my indecent embellishments, my discordant harmonies, my *deformis deformitas,* my tasselled parabolas, the dried flowers of my style ... And if my flowers are not dead, they are dying — which comes to the same thing.

I am not the heroic author of a "lapidary," of my epoch, nor of a "bestiary" (though the word bestial suits me well enough, I must admit); no, I am the author of a Summa of Sadness, and a Tractatus (apocryphal) on Woman — attributed as everyone knows to the great Theophrastus Bombast von Hohenheim.

Yes, I recognize that this book (my own, I mean) may well provoke some irritation, and infuriate the reader with its surfeit of unverifiable historical references. I know, too, that my disordered prose contains no ingredient of pleasure for the reader, or so little — and to so little purpose — that I feel in this respect like Saint Hildegarde with her preoccupation with the proportions of the human body. The *homo quadratus* that she had composed in the form of a perfect tetragon, cruciform, squared in his own geometric circle, Vitruvianized to death, was crucified!

The Antiphonary

But the orgasm of this ''squared man'' was not taken seriously, any more than the (indecent) orgasm of the tetragonal woman I was in Dr Franconi's arms. To hell with altimetry, planimetry, cosmimetry and profundimetry, if the gratification obtained (hastily and without morality) with a stranger makes a circle of me, inasmuch as it causes me to turn in an infinite spin and plunge into a bottomless gulf! I love the ecstasy of sex. Hideous, you say! But a few seconds of irresistible pleasure will always and infallibly prevail over the debilitating theories of Adam of Fulda and Ugolino of Orvieto.

After all that has happened I am inclined to believe in the theory of ugliness elaborated by Ulric of Strasbourg in the 13th century. What is filthy or corrupt, says the great Ulric, is more or less reducible to a lack of ontological quality, and this, in a differential way, allows us to attribute less beauty to certain entities, more to others. This relativism in embryo prompted Saint Augustine to say that the handsomest of apes is ugly when compared with man (a celebrated maxim which sums up in lapidary fashion the philosophy of ugliness).

Thus I, though beautiful, am paradoxically ugly (at least on the surface): degraded, sordid, punished, deformed, without *consonantia,* lacking in balance, I am a poor woman who admits the relativity of human love. I might even say that through my disorderly acts I profess my turpitude, which sums me up and defines me. I have, on this sinister morning, lived through the episode with Dr Franconi. I have even described it. What is more, that frightful business in the San Diego drugstore ... but you know all about that. You know too much about me. You know the closeups of my true and profound ugliness, my shame, the privation and poverty of my life ...

To tell the truth, I am aware of being a source of disillusionment: this is my strength and my vulnerability too: for, disappointing (present participle) to this degree, I may in the long run miss out on certain elocutionary effects that could confer a kind of scriptuary splendour on what I am doing (does my *via plana* end in the ancient *oratio dilucida et aperta*?). Is the overture I have begun reducible to a prothematic introduction, or is it rather a *modus dicendi* proper to me?

But everything is turning black ... I have a sudden feeling that my labia are thrusting into a shady epithalamion whose various characters (Jean-William, Robert, Dr Franconi, and finally myself ...) are dressed in bedtime costumes. Have you read the futile pages in which the great Chigi (alias Jean-William, alias Beausang, alias Leonardo da, alias Alfarabi) gives an irrefutable demonstration that the beauty of shadow (another discovery of the Renaissance, optical department) consists in attenuating or suppressing flaws or slight defects which would be made obvious by too bright a light? If you have not read these abstruse pages you have missed very little; shadow for shadow, mine are as valid and as dark as the distant shades which connoisseurs discern in the distances of the great Leonardo's paintings. My shadow equals my obscurity, and vice versa; and the former equals the latter. This darkness of the past is only an effect of our perception of it, because if one wished to see it in a lucid perspective this heap of blackness might resemble an agglomeration of sparkling stars or a warehouse of sacred ciboria. Why, after all, should I try to lead you astray — my reader, my sole and sombre reader — but why, on the other hand, should I oblige you to live through what I suffered? Why should I recreate for you the frightful scene that was my downfall? ... Here is a radical change: it is not useless to reveal even the most opaque of shades, any more than it would be useless to reveal that the face of the most wounded of all (Robert's) can be made — artificially — to conform to a circle, to an equilateral triangle, to a square or a pentagram. (Lorenzo Ghiberti affirms this, Villard de Honnecourt as well ...)

162

The Antiphonary

Well, as I was saying, here is the scene on wide screen with subtitles and technicolour tints: after all, I have to go into my act and describe what follows. First, so far as the sunrise scene is concerned, you know all you need to. Imagine now that after the obturation (blackout) of the screen, the lady star is shown in a long shot, dressing; then, zooming in to the left, we see dear Christine with her clothes on going up to the mirror on the medicine cabinet to do her makeup. Suddenly the star's expression (that's me still) shows that she is discouraged, troubled, disgusted with herself. She can't look at herself. Same focal distance, switch-pan to the office door of Dr Franconi, who goes out and slams the door shut behind him. Switch pan (again) to the mirror: a face going to pieces, a demogrification of the facial square, sad as death ... Christine is a poor creature rising after a test that has left its indelible mark upon her. Any ambiguity in the last phrase is quite intentional. But what does it matter, after all ... Second blackout on the superscreen: utter darkness, unrelieved, then full lights and Robert's room, a long shot, with Dr Franconi making a majestic entrance from left to right across the screen (I feel that I should speed up the movement, but I cannot: for me, Dr Franconi can enter a patient's room in no other way but slowly and majestically). Cut to Robert, himself cut by intravenous entries in his wrists and ankles (4 in all), seemingly dead. Dr Franconi solemnly enters the frame. The nurse hands him the report. The doctor runs through it slowly, lingering over the temperature and blood pressure variations of his patient. As he reads, the nurse turns, surprised, toward the door. It seems someone has made a noisy entrance on the scene. It's Christine! Cut to closeup of me, sweating, anxious (no lines to say), then looking suddenly at the doctor (the celebrated Dr Franconi). By a trick of framing the two faces (the doctor's and mine) are close to each other ...

I'm going to have to use some other technique; the scene

163

is dislocated by this inharmonious, incoherent perspective I'm using ...

I now continue with the panoramic recall of this sequence in the room of the badly wounded man. Dr Franconi turns coldly toward me and says:

"I'm not sure he can be saved. In any case I must inform you that your husband, Mr Bernatchez, must recover consciousness within the next 48 hours. If not — if not, he is lost."

"Will you still operate?"

"Yes," said Dr Franconi, "and I must begin at once. Would you be good enough to wait, either in the waiting room or, if you wish, in my office? Here, take the key. You know where it is ... "

(Imperturbable, he looked away from me and began to give instructions to the nurse, who took careful note. I — well, I went out without looking back. Perhaps I'll never see Robert alive again. I left the room with this terrifying thought, despairing, and went on my way, not to the celebrated Dr Franconi's office but toward the main exit. The weather outside was superb. It was 4 in the morning and the sunlight cast a luminous mist over the world. Never had the trees along the Rivière des Prairies seemed to me so invitingly dusky, the sky so profoundly blue and soft, the air so good to breathe. I walked some distance without thinking where I was going, but this mattered little for I was exhilarated by the profusive power of the light and the calm of the whole decor (*decora moderatio,* Cassiodorus would have said). Yes, I had a kind of urge to fill my lungs with the gentle and already warm air of this summer morning. Moreover my walk, after four days of seclusion, took my mind off that torture chamber where Robert was dying by slow degrees (oh God! ... slow?). And was he really going to die, or would he be reborn and come back to me as handsome as he was, as loving as he had been at the Auberge de l'Etoile? It was better to walk for ever, north, east, west or south, than ask myself these obsessive questions ... Yes, I should walk, walk, walk and keep on walking, while Robert underwent a delicate operation in the fragile networks of the conticothalamic region ...)

If I intervene — at this moment — in my own story, it is merely because I am particularly and intensely conscious just now of adopting a disorganized and even irritating style (though recounting things that happened such a short time ago). A few sentences back I dropped in a quote from Cassiodorus and it would have been better — this I readily admit — to have restrained myself from doing so. But — how can I explain? — I haven't got much of a style, I don't *write* with style, and this probably explains the sinister graphic spasmophilia in which I'm indulging; an outsider might think I was distorting myself, exploding, in fission, disintegrating, pulverizing myself into a host of atonal and cross-hatched series of words or symbols; in fact, like a nebula, I am streaking through a liquefied stratosphere in a dead and bottomless sea (its surface turbulent with howling winds). In other words — such as might be used by Dr Franconi (that learned erectile monster) — I believe that I am shaken by a series of schematic hylozomorphic shocks, developing in serial feed-back ... I should stop here, I know, but can I? Have I the skill to use the rhetorical devices of Cornaficius as Dr Franconi uses — for one thing — his scalpel? One more drop of this and the reader will be disgusted: there, I've done it, I'm displeasing, irritating; I give pain, I'm a headache. Yes, it's an implacable process, inevitable, but quite unpredictable, one that will categorize me for whatever literary critic may have to deal with a *compositio* like mine. He'll say — the critic will say — that ... Well, I think what he writes will have to take into account that I did do my best to tell the truth. I have white-washed nothing, distorted nothing, exaggerated nothing. That fit which

The Antiphonary

Jean-William had in San Diego, believe me, was the most atrocious I have ever been privileged to see (and, from my own point of view, the most painful). The incident that took place that evening in the druggist's dispensary, and the tragic consequences of that incident — these were all things that happened just as I described them! And now it's all falling back on me, influencing me in return like a soaring breaker pounding at my kidneys! The result is, I let myself go, I write like a drowning creature, I strangle, I suffocate. The words I used in capsules at the beginning melt and run strangely alongside of me in this burlesque fiesta which I tried to see as tragedy! In a few hours, if this goes on, I will kill myself without taking any precautions ... But then ...

(Day was slipping gently toward its appointed shadowy end when I returned, exhausted, to Sacré-Coeur hospital. I had passed the intervening hours wandering through the streets of Cartierville and Ahuntsic and now was dead with fatigue, my mind empty, when I finally made my appearance in the usual corridor that led to Robert's room. A nurse took my arm and, without saying a word, led me into a kind of library where other nurses were silently consulting various medical journals.

"What's the matter," I asked.

" ...."

"No, wait a second, — I'm out of breath ..."

" ...."

"Well, out with it, for heaven's sake! Has something serious happened??? Robert!!! Is he ... dead??"

"No, no, and please don't be so loud. Here's what happened: a certain Mr Forestier came here and asked to see your husband, Mr Bernatchez. I had no idea ..."

"Jean-William!!! Oh, no! Did he try to kill him?"

"Yes. He took a pistol from his jacket pocket and waved it in the direction of Mr Bernatchez' heart. He was just going to shoot when I rushed at him. He slipped and fell hard against the door of the sickroom. His pistol skidded across the floor. I dove for the gun, trying to beat him to it ... and made it ..."

"Well, go on!"

"Yes. Your husband, Mr Bernatchez, was just coming out of his coma. He saw Mr Forestier." She was suddenly almost in tears, and I along with her.

"You see ... he took in the whole thing, and it brought on a very serious relapse — but don't worry about his safety ... Mr Forestier managed to get away, even though there were several orderlies after him. He was very fast, they said. And now your husband's room is being guarded by two detectives from the Montreal police, so don't worry. And ... I think your husband's doing a little better."

"I must see him."

"No, Mrs Bernatchez, that's strictly forbidden. Dr Franconi is using electrical reanimation."

"Then that means ... that ..." (I didn't dare finish the sentence.)

"Yes," the nurse replied.

"But where can I go?" I asked her.

"Just follow me, please."

I fell into step behind her. She walked very fast, taking stairs and corridors unfamiliar to me, and left me, believe it nor not, in Dr Franconi's office.

"Whatever happens," she said, "you'll have the least to fear if you're here. And you can be sure I'll let you know if there's good news. Here, take this pill. Dr Franconi asked me to give it to you half an hour before bedtime."

"What's in it?"

"I don't know. Just a second. Here's a glass of water."

I swallowed the sky-blue pill. I don't remember anything after

167

The Antiphonary

that.

The Antiphonary

The time has come for me to give an account of myself, but I'm wandering about in a finicky description of Leonico Chigi's activities in Lyon, and find that infinitely more entertaining than going on with this book, which is killing me. Imagine our dear defrocked abbot finding in Lyon a new, safe and fascinating life, an ample reward for his crime committed in Geneva! Irony of fate: for him, crime at first paid, and very generously. In the beginning he passed his time composing short tales in the manner of the age, then turned again to the text of Jules-César Beausang, which so far as we can judge he enriched with several passages from his own hand (Chigi's). He was an accomplished artist in all the techniques of writing, but though Chigi set himself to inventing fictitious stories, he seems to me to have succeeded better by far in his autobiography. This technique came to him, perhaps, from the daily reading of his breviary (at the rate of one chapter a day), for it was one of fragmentation. Chigi composed his autobiographical story in several fragments (or tableaux) only half-connected one to the other, dislocated, disjointed. The whole gives a strong impression of discontinuity; brutally choppy. Nothing could be stranger than this discordant style which breaks instead of building, tearing down as it goes the little that has been allowed to stand. To my notion, the procedure is a perfectly satisfying and effective way of going about a book on any subject whatsoever. It can be applied in a scientific treatise or a book of fiction and the reader will in no way be inconvenienced because of the fragmentary method. At least, that is my very naive conviction. Could I be identifying with Chigi's method because his atomized view of reality and his way of expressing it suit me in a personal way? Of course. I am a fragmentalist, so to speak, and in no way inclined toward a spherical representation of reality. Existence for me is merely a series of broken sequences, each sufficient to itself, and the sum of all the parts is never equal to a whole. In fact, totality (that mystical plenitude whose function is doubtless to compensate for the disorder and frustration of non-plenitude — the void . . .) has no reality except as a model created by the mind (*cf.* gestalt psychology). I conceive that I myself, for that matter, am involved in an endless process of totalization, and that, proceeding by fragments, I will never attain totality or plenitude (worse still: I'm getting farther from it, diverging, breaking loose). And now, with all this I've given the slip to poor Chigi in the silken maze of the great city of the Rhone, in somewhat the same way that I'm going on to lose myself (in the second degree) through my own narcissism (showing off my theories to the reader). But back to Lyon: Chigi lives very simply there. Every morning (at about 7:00) he leaves for the press, he works there until about the 4th hour in winter (the 5th in summer), *i.e.* until 11:00 or noon. Then, after a frugal meal eaten at the shop with his co-workers, he continues to work until sundown. This goes on six days a week. In exchange, Vascosan pays him 4 ducats a month plus some trifling monthly gift, such as a silver ring with a secret hollow in the setting, a smelling-box (commonly used at the time), a hinged collar, a tortoise-shell snuffbox, a soup-bowl, a sauce-dish of silver with no hallmark, three goblets of an alloy of copper and silver, a silver chafing-dish . . . etc. As we can see, these little gifts (which Chigi cherished and described for us in detail) give a very precise notion of what Vascosan gave as a supplement to his pay. Chigi — or so I believe — received these articles in silver as remuneration for the texts he wrote himself to be later printed and distributed by Vascosan: guide-books, translations, adaptations, plagiarisms, prayer books, putative texts by Jules-César Beausang (or anyone you care to name). Lewd tales, and so on. But Vascosan's operations were numerous and profitable, if we judge by the kind of bonus given to certain of his employees.

Moreover, life in Lyon represented for Chigi the *summum* of refinement and civilization. In his diary he never tires of praising the many restaurants he was privileged to visit with V. (Vascosan, I imagine) and his wife, or on occasion with other friends whom he does not name but who had known Etienne Dolet and talked a great deal about him. But their remarks as noted by Chigi do not add much new material to what we know about Dolet, whether from various works of historiography or from Dolet himself. The famous heretic, burned, of course, in 1537, left a fabulous image of himself. He was considered after his death as the "first martyr of the Reformation" — a title he has kept to our day. Chigi mentions his case as a curiosity, for he himself, though he had abjured the faith right and left in Geneva (with Antonella), could in no way be described as a supporter of Calvin or Luther. At times he has a word of admiration for Bucer, with compliments for his sense of proportion and his "resemblance to Erasmus of Rotterdam," the great Christian humanist of Basel who, at the end of his life, took refuge in London for his greater safety. Erasmus, I must say, has never excited my imagination. Everyone knows he was prudent (and classed as a "humanist" because of it); but was prudence ever the great syncretic virtue that allowed a man to outclass all his contemporaries? I think not.

But there I go again, jumping from Chigi to Erasmus and, Lord knows, perhaps next to Witelo, famous for his book *Perspective* or perhaps to a certain English monk, victim of the Black Death in Munich in 1549 and author of a well-known *Tractatus de Successivis* (in which we find an exposition of his great theory of motion — an ingenious one which was taken up in part by Galileo and Kepler). You may say that the *Venerabilis inceptor* has no pertinence to the gloomy story I have undertaken to set down, proceeding as best I can along the paths of narrative technique. Of course, you are perfectly right! And I would stop there, breathless, naked, discomfited! But in truth Swineshead and Heytesbury are equally irrevelant to my theme, not to mention a certain Adam Goddam (died 1501 after raping a nun!). Again you would be right: if we face facts, the reality I am attempting through words to make my own escapes me and leaves me empty-handed, I lose my hold upon it and grope in all directions, as if suddenly some unmentionable element in my story had depolarized me and confined me to the defocalizing confusion of simple grief.

The Antiphonary

"How beautiful are thy feet with shoes, O prince's daughter! The joints of thy thighs are like jewels, the work of the hands of a cunning workman. Thy navel is like a round goblet, which wanteth not liquid ... Thy two breasts are like two young roes that are twins. Thy neck is as a tower of ivory; thine eyes like the fish-pools of Heshbon, by the gate of Bath-rabbim. Thy nose is as the tower of Lebanon which looketh toward Damascus ... How fair and how pleasant art thou, O love, for delights! This thy stature is like to a palm tree, and thy breasts to clusters of grapes. I said, I will go up to the palm tree, I will take hold of the boughs thereof; now also thy breasts shall be as clusters of the vine, and the smell of thy nose like apples ..."

These words fill me with a kind of euphoric enchantment. Each time I re-read them or, as now, reproduce their detailed denominations and their endless reiterations, I have an impression of physical ecstasy, almost a climax felt in solitude and despair. I don't know how else to describe this ineffable joy that sets me divinely afire and at the same time confers on me a clearer than normal vision of life and love.

Ever since Jean-William gave me this edition of the Bible, published by the American Bible Society in 1826 (in New York), I have never left the precious book far from my hand, reading and re-reading it, always with the same interior passion. He found this rare edition in an antique shop in Santa Barbara. A forgotten book, one would have said. It was lying on the dusty shelves of the antique store, among other more or less old editions of English or American books. I remember that the same dealer had two volumes of the first edition of Macaulay's *History of England*. As there are five in the complete work it would have been a bad buy to take it as it was, incomplete. At the same time (while Jean-William was poking around among the books) I was trying to find something, some little thing, to give him. There were all kinds of cufflinks (none to make a matching pair, which infuriated me) and old fob-watches, extra-flat, which had doubtless belonged to rich Americans for they were all made in Europe. Only one thing had appealed to me: an old cowboy revolver with a silver-plated barrel and mother-of-pearl grip. A real gem of an antique, but he wanted a hundred dollars for it, and that held me back.

This revolver no doubt prefigured in Jean-William's subconscious the homicidal weapon he was to use (a few days later, in San Diego) to murder the druggist. And don't think for a moment that I normally follow this kind of semi-occult reasoning; in fact, I have no faith in it whatsoever. When I was in the antique shop with Jean-William in Santa Barbara I had no inkling that I was a few days from being savagely beaten by him, or that I would leave him for fear of being killed. I hadn't the slightest idea of what was to follow, *i.e.* the horrible sequence of events that I'm trying to present in some kind of order (arbitrary), but which really were characterized by their utter unpredictability and chaotic sequence. No more had I any idea that I would now be in Dr Franconi's office (in the hospital), waiting patiently — five whole days — for Robert, the man I love, my only love, to come out of his comatose condition. My God! I certainly had no premonition of all that!

Five days. Five whole days now that I've been living in this hospital, two steps from the man they are trying to reanimate (in vain, so far) after he was gravely wounded by Jean-William. One can try all one likes to conjure up horrors, one could never predict this kind of event, a masterpiece of black irony and confusion (Jean-William's attack on Robert)!

After his visit yesterday (I mean Jean-William's appearance at his victim's bedside during my walk through the streets of Montreal), Jean-William disappeared again. No doubt he's waiting somewhere to strangle me. Yes, he's waiting for Robert to leave the hospital and this time he'll kill him with his bare hands (for Jean-William no longer has the weapon in question). Moreover, he's been identified (this time I was obliged to go through with it, his height, his address, colour of hair, eyes, address of parents, as well as names and addresses of certain friends or relatives where he might be likely to hide out. I had to do this, for the inspector who questioned me about him forced me to tell him everything, or else, as he said, he would have no choice but to accuse me of complicity). So now that the police have all the information I gave them, Jean-William can't escape too much longer from the mills of justice. He is being sought by the whole police force — he must be. Sooner or later he's going to catch the eye of some policeman, who'll tail him and then simply arrest him and slap on the handcuffs.

There's just nothing. Robert's neither better nor worse. Dr Franconi hasn't been back in his office since the other day. I'm beginning to worry seriously about his staying away, for I feel it has some connection with Robert's getting worse and the Doctor's professional embarrassment about the whole thing. The nurse told me a while ago that she would come and see me about 9 o'clock this evening. It's time now and she hasn't come. I'm waiting. That's all I do in life this last while. All the stuff about Beausang and Chigi — making a fortune with adulterated texts in Lyon — is coming out my ears. Sometimes I read a little from the book Chigi wrote but, really, I don't feel involved any more, I'm just not interested the way I was before. My life has changed to the point where I've lost all desire to make a success of it by writing my thesis. My mind has never been farther from working on that thesis, and I never cared less about making a success of my life. I've probably ruined everything, and for good. So, how can I rescue anything? Even Robert, reunited with me in spite of everything, will perhaps leave me soon, courtesy of a minor but fatal faltering of the cardiac function ...

She came (the nurse) at 9:35. She told me Robert had a chance, that I shouldn't despair, that he was in good hands. Then she gave me the pill (a powerful sedative) and a glass of water. She saw it down before she left. I just swallowed it. I sleep naked, in a state of complete euphoria from this drug prescribed by Dr Franconi. "I am black but comely, O ye daughters of Jerusalem, as the tents of Kedar, as the curtains of Solomon ... I sat down under his shadow with great delight, and his fruit was sweet to my taste. He brought me to the banqueting house, and his banner over me was love. Stay me with flagons, comfort me with apples, for I am sick of love. His left hand is under my head, and his right hand doth embrace me ... Daughters of Jerusalem, I am sick of love ..."

I'm falling asleep, the Bible I was reading in bed has fallen from my hands. I see my writing falter and my hand tremble, and now, delicately — secretly, under the freshly-washed sheets — I touch the lower part of my body. My belly is really changed! It's obvious the druggist left a living trace of himself in me, in my womb. Strange, my clitoris seems to wilt under the pressure of my finger. My vagina no longer emits the visceral liquid that is a sign of gratification. Sleep is dulling my senses completely. Tomorrow, tomorrow ...

The Antiphonary

It happened with the speed of lightning. I was fighting my way slowly out of my drugged sleep in this bed installed in Dr Franconi's office, when he delicately made his presence known to me. I don't really know how it happened without my waking, but when I did become conscious Dr Franconi was turning down the blanket with which I had covered my nudity. He was behind me, lying on the bed, as naked as I was, and already erect inside me, without so much as a by-your-leave.

"You were sleeping," he said softly, when he saw that I was awake.

"What's that drug you gave me yesterday, and the night before as well?"

"It's a sedative that's very light and easy to eliminate from the system, don't worry. Tell me, I'd be interested to know if you had any dreams while you slept?"

"No, Doctor, no." I was almost struck dumb by his calm and his beauty — which I hadn't noticed the first time.

"Are you very sleepy just now?"

"No, no," I said again — but I was thinking of the eulogy of the beloved, and the languor of the verse from the Song of Songs that I had read before going to sleep.

"I didn't want to surprise you. I hope you weren't frightened? Tell me ..."

"No ... How can I say it? I'm not frightened, but somehow I'm confused and a little embarrassed. I don't really know the reason!" I said.

The Antiphonary

"If you're worried about your husband, let me reassure you.
I think he'll survive, and he may even recover consciousness
sometime today."

"Really? Oh, I'm so pleased, I'm so relieved."

"My ... presence here at this moment shouldn't bother you
too much in any case. Last time I may have thought too much
of my own pleasure at finding you and contemplating you, and
I may have been a shade brusque and clumsy, was I?"

"Doctor, you know very well I'm uneasy and even feel guilty
... because ..."

"Believe me, little lady, you needn't feel any undue guilt
about your husband."

"Why do you say that?"

"Well," replied the Doctor, "I'll tell you the whole story.
The whole story. Here," he said, as if in passing, "come over
like this, you'll feel more comfortable, you'll see."

(He turned me over and there I was — oh shame! — on
top of him ...)

"Now," he went on, "it would be nonsense to feel much
guilt if you, say, were unfaithful to him with me, for Mr Bernatchez when he's cured will most likely be unable to experience
physical union with you."

"What! What's this you're telling me?" As I said these words
I was struggling to push him away, escape his embrace, get
away from his body, for I suddenly hated him for saying that
about Robert. (It was strange, at that time I tended to hold him
responsible for anything of the kind happening to Robert.)

"Come, come," he said, "don't be like that, all nervous and
stiff with me."

I started crying, shedding great tears, holding nothing back,
sad beyond measure. This irresistible sadness (which I'd been
keeping more or less to myself until then) came over me with
a flood of warm tears that ran down my cheeks and sprinkled

the face of Dr Franconi, who was still holding me solidly on top of him.

"Now, now, don't let yourself go like that," he said. "I'm here, and I'll help you if you let me. Seriously, I will help you in any way I can."

"But you told me Robert would get well," I said, sobbing, "and now he'll be impotent for the rest of his days! Impotent! Poor Robert! I just wonder if you're not using me cynically . . . " and I started sobbing harder than ever, and that seemed to do me good, I don't know why.

"I've told you the truth," said the Doctor. "I thought that was better than a nice-sounding lie. Was I wrong?"

"I'm sorry. Just let me cry a little for Robert, let me get it out of my system; life is so unfair!"

"If you really want," said Dr Franconi gently, "I'll leave you for a while. I think that may be best, because this has been a terrible shock for you. I'm not inhuman, you know!"

He made a move as if to withdraw from me, leave me alone . . .

"Doctor!" I said, holding him close — for I didn't want him to leave me at a time like that —" tell me the whole truth. I really want to know everything. Robert is going to be impotent — but what else? Are you keeping anything else as serious from me?"

"My poor dear," he said, "I don't know. I truly don't know. I've been wondering myself if organic lesions will leave him handicapped later. You know, head lesions; well, they're very serious wounds, for they affect certain delicate regions where all the nervous systems of the body converge."

"Well?"

"Don't ask me too much. I can't even tell you the consequences of his cranial traumatism or all the operations. I just don't know."

"At the worst," I said, "what could become of him? I mean

179

the worst, supposing Robert is seriously affected?''

The Doctor took his time thinking over his answer. I felt that he was loath to carry on our talk on this subject, and had no inclination — this time — to be cynical. I found this far from reassuring. What was more, he suddenly began to extract himself from me. I believe he no longer wanted me, felt no desire. I drew back softly and turned on my right side, with my back to him. My tears ran down in silence onto the immaculate, wrinkled sheet. My partner had detached himself completely. The seconds or minutes seemed interminable, heavy, unbearably heavy . . .

"Impotent!" I repeated mechanically. "Robert will be impotent the rest of his life."

"I think I can speak frankly to you, for you deserve it," he said, very softly. "Your husband — or so I fear, for him and for you — your husband, at the worst, as you say, may suffer a hemiplegia, that is, a paralysis of some cranial nerves on the side where the lesion is, and a hemiplegia of the limbs on the opposite side."

I stopped weeping and listened.

"Let me go on," said the Doctor. "As you learned at medical school, this alternate hemiplegia can set in when the lesion is located at a bulbous or peduncular level where the fibres of the pyramidal fasciculus have already undergone decussation."

"Is that so in Robert's case?" I asked, no longer crying.

"It's a borderline case, shall we say," Dr Franconi replied. "But if not, I'm afraid he might be suffering from an attenuated Brown-Sequard syndrome, though that is hardly likely."

"And what then?"

"Well," said the Doctor, "don't you know the rest?"

"The wheel chair. Is that it?" I asked. I was far from tears now. Suddenly I felt myself receding from the whole horrible business. Yet I was shattered about Robert. I think I'd rather have heard just then that he had passed away.

"Yes, the wheel chair. I mean, at the very worst," said the Doctor.

"Poor Robert," I said aloud and (as I thought) without emotion.

"I think I'll leave you alone," said the Doctor. "I just hope you'll forgive me a little for my cynicism the other time?"

I turned toward him again, looking deep into his blue eyes. Suddenly he seemed much more human, almost tender, as if he were touched. Finally I could look quietly at him — without any internal conflict, with no feelings of guilt. I laid my head on his chest, leaning heavily against him. He took my hand affectionately, caressed the back of my neck. Strangely enough, I no longer felt ashamed, but liberated, freed at last!

Need I relate what happened between us? I think not. A spontaneous flood of words of love, a wave of caresses, a happening that seemed to me most beautiful and rich, filled with generous feelings and stamped with melancholy.

The Antiphonary

"Thou art beautiful, O my love, as Tirzah, comely as Jerusalem, terrible as an army with banners. Turn thine eyes from me, for they have overcome me. Thy hair is as a flock of goats that appear from Gilead. Thy teeth are as a flock of sheep that go up from the washing ... As a piece of pomegranate are the temples within thy locks ... Return, return, O Shulamite, return, return ..."

This passage from the Song of Songs, so dear to Chigi who had lost his Shulamite, he recopied and re-read a hundred times, no doubt, in secret in his attic room, in the evening, by his candle. But his intimate diary ends abruptly. Chigi had been describing in detail his possessions in silver plate and copper, how he passed his time at the printer's, how he missed Antonella and his regrets when he thought of his misconduct, then, brutally, after the description of a fine dinner at Tête de Cerf, a restaurant on the outskirts of Lyon (near Cullins), Leonico Chigi tells us about a strange itching desire of his, and about certain acquaintances having caught the Great Pox (syphilis) after sleeping with bohemian women, and he wonders if he too will not succumb to the much-vaunted charms of these famous nomadic ladies. He has already met one or two on his way to the printer's (his place of work). He is stunned by their beauty, their brown pigmentation, their blue eyes full of voluptuous promise. Then, at home, writing up his diary, he is one day away from his monthly pay and his usual bonus (proportional no doubt to the number of faked and adulterated lines he has produced). He is undecided.

The Antiphonary

We share his hesitation. He wonders whether, this time, he should treat himself to a feast at a fine restaurant, Au Renard (near Saint-Etienne, outside of town), or if it wouldn't be better to pay off his debts ... or even save the money for going back to Turin or maybe Lugano (where he could live incognito).

Chigi's hesitation does not last long, at least in the text itself. A dozen lines: then nothing, silence, death. According to the testimony of a contemporary, our dear Zimara feasted not in the Renard but elsewhere (he thinks he recalls that it was an inn at Charbonnières, which had been incorporated into the city). After this fabulous meal Zimara (alias Chigi) is said to have recited to this confidant and friend certain verses from the Song of Songs and from Ecclesiastes, for hours on end, alluding with increasing frequency to the Shulamite of Geneva, dropping Antonella's name from time to time. Then Zimara (or the pseudo-Zimara) begged his friend to go with him to the gypsy women (who, according to him, possessed a beauty typically Shulamitic), with whom he was bound and determined to experience the secret miracles and marvels of love they were supposed to perform. His friend enjoined him not to give in to this mad desire, suggesting instead the solid compensations of the professionals of Lyon. But our good Zimara-Chigi wouldn't let go his notion. Come what might, he wanted to know the folly and joy of life, in a wild concatenation of drink, debauchery and excess of all kinds. He was found several weeks later in quarantine at the Hôtel-Dieu in Lyon (at least so says our anonymous informer), a victim of the Great Pox which was, some say, the "mal du siècle."

Chigi's sordid end leaves me completely cold. What do I care if he died of syphilis after sleeping with the gypsies of Lyon, or some other way? He interests me no longer. This dear spoiled priest is not only a matter of indifference to me; he irritates me seriously, now that you mention it, and the very thought of him revolts me. I couldn't tell you why. Probably because

The Antiphonary

I have no heart for anything. My personal lack fills me with a general demoralization which invades my noetic field. I have become paralyzed by the injustice of life, the sordid side of recent events (Jean-William's attempt on Robert's life, Robert's days in hospital, his coma, (about to end) and my own confinement to a cramped, tiny office where I have lost all dignity and self-respect etc.). I realize that Robert will never know I have been unfaithful to him with his doctor, nor how often or under what circumstances. Of course, I will never talk about this particular matter. The other (I mean, the Doctor) will also keep his mouth shut. And Robert will come back to a woman who apparently stayed faithful to him, who shows no premonitory signs of a growing divorce from reality, and who will never leave him. He will find in me a faithful companion, tender and helpful in his convalescence, careful also to spare him any reminders or memories of frightening or painful events. I shall be gentle with him, I will help him into his wheel chair and push it myself, and then, in the evening, I will be his helper in the operation of getting into bed (for that, alas, will never be easy). I also know I will have to administer a certain number of medicaments having to do with his ambulatory therapy: constrictors, SNC stimulants, various hemostatics (in tablet form), digitalis, veal liver extract, and whatnot. I will have a list, I will know what to do and when. I'll never let him out of my sight. But when I do go out to shop I will be obliged to put certain neuroleptic products under lock and key, and any instrument that could be used to slash or strangle. I know all this. I even know that he will never have an erection, and therefore no orgasm. I may have to resign myself to masturbating him so that he has some pleasure, from time to time. But would it be medically sound to provoke an orgasm, however feeble, in that body? I don't know ... My God! — when my baby arrives I will need some care too. And Robert will be helpless! ... I will have to go

184

to hospital to have it, most likely; no, most certainly! And he'll
be alone in the house. Impossible! For the last three months,
I'd say, my sister Viviane — what a pity, she lives in LaSarre
— will have to come and help me with Robert. She could feed
him, help him with his other needs, lift him into bed, keep
him company . . . How else could I do it? If not Viviane (married,
two children in school) I'll have to find a maid or a nurse. Oh
Lord, when I think all this over I realize the incredible extent
to which Robert's existence will be out of phase with mine.
I can't believe it! I shudder already. Robert will be a fraction
of a man, no longer himself, a man diminished, self-effacing,
perhaps suicidal (or: obsessed by some suicidal project). He will
never again be able to hold a responsible position or deal with
important affairs or get around from place to place with ease.
Just putting him into a car will be a major undertaking, not
to mention airplanes: that will be completely out of the question.
We'll have to dismiss any thought of it. I must talk all this
over with Dr Franconi. But with him I know in advance what
will happen, and by what subtle changes of tempo and atmosphere
we will end up doing what we have done each time we were
alone any length of time. I sometimes think I may be responsible
for what happened, for in fact I provoked his excitement —
at least the first time. It's frightful. It's unspeakable! I am more
afraid of myself than I am of him! I don't recognize myself
any more. How can one ever tell? I've become another woman.
Or I am going mad, going to pieces. There is nothing honourable
left about me. I don't know how to stop, what with everything
that's happened since San Diego.

There is no more morality in my behaviour with other men.
The more I go on like this, the more I'm sure Jean-William
struck me, beat me, because all at once he despised me totally.
In his eyes I was already a whore, a bitch in heat, a creature
unworthy of respect. Since that time — paradoxically — I seem

to be conforming to his image of me. My behaviour horrifies
me, I am ashamed . . .

The Antiphonary

He gets out tomorrow around 10. (And Jean-William is still at large. No policeman has laid the heavy hand on his shoulder . . .)

The Antiphonary

I miss Jean-William. Seriously, deeply, I feel his absence as a terrible privation. I know that he struck me, beat me, treated me frightfully — but only because I deserved no better ... God, I should silence in myself this immodest desire I feel for Jean-William. It's quite intolerable, this feeling of missing a naked body that one has caressed and kissed, that marvellous body whose indefatigable elasticity and potency I know so well! I would do vile things to have him inside me again, to have him undress me not worrying whether he tore this or that. Yes I would ask him, if he were in his right mind, to roll on top of me, to crush me with his weight, to suck my breasts and hold them in his hands, to caress my belly, kiss me on one ear then the other, and then massage me, as he did so well, on the soft inside of my thighs! This is madness. I'm delirious, obsessed with obscene hallucinations from that cursed drug Franconi gives me! And at the same time I'm completely unfair to Robert. I feel no pity for him, I have no desire to see him again, I'd leave him to the transfusions that are keeping him alive, just to go away with Jean-William, who, after all this time without me, would possess me once more before he took my life. For I know very well he would kill me, that he would never forgive me for having left him like a coward in San Diego and come back to Montreal to take up again with Robert and live together with him — the little time, that is, that we managed to live together ... I think this time I cannot hesitate to finish what I intended doing. I have a few hours left and strength

188

enough for that. ''Let us die and enter into darkness,'' said Saint Bonaventure somewhere. A bittersweet exhortation which I never understood before!

POSTFACE

I was in tears when I read the end of Christine's manuscript. A month has gone by since then, and many events as well, many stirring events. The day she wrote the last word of her book she took her own life. To do so she used a technique known to few besides doctors and nurses: she took a syringe from the instruments in a case in that little office in Sacré-Coeur hospital, and gave herself an intravenous injection which produced a gaseous embolism. She was found lying on the hospital bed that had been set up in that office, the syringe still hanging from her flesh. She died in a few seconds. During this time Robert was still floating in his coma, unconscious, still in a critical condition. He regained consciousness half-way through the following night, while a nurse called Landry was at his bedside . . . At once she called the desk and the doctor on duty (I forget his name), after which she phoned here directly to speak to Albert. I didn't like that too much, it seemed very odd to me. How did they know at the hospital that Albert was here? I hesitated, then decided finally to shake Albert awake. He was sleeping very soundly.

"What is it?" he asked grumpily.

"An emergency call, from the hospital."

"All right, give it to me . . . ."

He took the phone, still half asleep, peevish, a little irritated at being called in the middle of the night.

"Franconi here," he said gruffly.

I was already resigned to seeing him go off in his car in

the dead of night, driving, half asleep, to Cartierville, when I heard him give a cry of surprise.

"What????!!!!"

I asked him what was wrong.

"In the next two minutes you'll get a serum transfusion going ... I'll be there in ..."

Covering the phone with his hand he whispered, "Your husband, he's just come out of his coma."

"Well," I said coldly, "do I have to tell you what to do in a case like this?"

"Sorry, Suzanne, I'm sorry." And he went on to the nurse: "... fifteen minutes, let's say. I'll be right there."

He hung up. He remained a few seconds near me, not saying a word. He seemed troubled, embarrassed toward me.

"Albert," I said, taking his hand, "you don't expect me to ask you to let him die on purpose? Don't worry, I know that deontological reasons oblige you to act as if he were just anyone. I'll make you a cup of instant coffee while you're getting ready."

And I went out to the kitchen where, two minutes later, he followed me, fumbling at his tie.

"Here," I said, holding out his coffee cup, "and take good care on the freeway. It would really be too much if you died trying to save him."

We both tried to smile despite the circumstances. Then Albert went quickly without saying a word.

What followed is very simple. I am the only living part of the tableau. Jean-William was killed in a car accident, near Saint-Lazare. It had all the marks of a suicide. Robert slowly regained consciousness, after which he wanted to come back with me. I let him know I was not the least interested in looking after cripples! This frightful conversation (the last one with Robert) was only two days ago. I asked him how he was. He told me all his wounds and ailments. And I said to him, "I suppose your little Christine is looking after you?''

Poor Robert, he put up a desperate fight. He didn't know how to word things so as to make me understand enough without giving away too much. But I knew everything (too bad for him). I left him hanging with not a twinge of pity, nary a touch of pity or tolerance.

''You were unfaithful to me,'' I said to him, ''and you can pay for your infidelity ... Robert,'' I said to him, ''I never want to see you again.''

He was pitiful on the other end of the line. I could hear him puffing and weeping and muttering all kinds of shapeless cries and calls for help. Pitiless; I remained pitiless!

What a heap of beastliness life is! I can't get over it. It's horrible. I sent Robert packing, back to his Christine, who had been unfaithful to him in the most shameless way with Albert (whom she calls in her manuscript ''Doctor Franconi,'' a respectful form of address that hardly suits Christine); for my own part, I remembered that Albert had welcomed me to his apartment after Robert went off with Christine, and that if only for this gesture he deserved nothing less than my fidelity and total attachment. If my desire to remain faithful to Albert needs any justification (in his eyes) I will tell him that my love for him goes back to a time in my life (two years ago) when our encounters, on Tuesday afternoons in the Queen Elizabeth, filled me with a ''sacred love'' which, by definition, is eternal.

But Christine crossed my path again! The manuscript I've just read taught me many things I might have died without knowing! Strange, the thing I found most shattering was her allusion to San Mateo and South San Francisco (as if she had gone there after the San Diego incident), for I myself lived through worse than hell in those peripheral municipalities of San Francisco (San Mateo and S.S.F.) during the trip Albert and I made together in the hope of getting back his two daughters (by his first marriage;

he had not seen them for four or five years). My God! — as
Christine would say — Albert and I had undertaken the trip
to the Pacific on the advice of a private investigation agency.
In fact, it was through this agency that we knew where Albert's
two daughters and their mother were (she had remarried under
the name of Mrs E. Taylor) in San Francisco. It was a dramatic
situation. When we arrived we went to the city itself, south
of Golden Gate Park, a charming neighbourhood where his former
wife was living. By evening we knew the exact house, and the
next day we returned to wait for the two girls. But that was
a school holiday in San Francisco. The next day was Saturday,
then came Sunday — nothing we could do. On Monday, Albert,
in his car at the corner of 29th Avenue and the Park, was waiting
for his two daughters to see what time they left for school. All
this time I waited, in bed in the International Motel in South
San Francisco, ready to leave like a flash with Albert and his
two daughters and dash to the airport — situated near the International Motel in the municipality of South San Francisco.

I thought Alfred would never get back from the city, in the
Ford-Galaxy 500 (sky blue) which we had rented. I was restless,
holed up in that motel-room, desperately waiting for a phone-call
telling me he had arrived with his two daughters. He came back
to the motel around 5 p.m., weeping, unable to say a word,
throwing himself on the bed without speaking to me.

I gathered he had been unsuccessful, but I learned only later,
among the thickets of Brisbane (the following day), that Albert
had left his car to walk toward his two little daughters, and
that they, to his great surprise, had not known him. The older
one, Renée, took to her heels and ran to warn her mother about
the strange man (Albert), while he, on the sidewalk, tried to
strike up a conversation with Claudette (9) who had the greatest
possible trouble replying to him in proper French — for both
of them go to an English school. The ex-wife (Mrs Taylor) came

The Antiphonary

out to the street and dragged her daughter away from Albert, with whom she herself immediately struck up a violent quarrel, hurling all kinds of insults and threats at him, until the neighbours, alerted by her cries and the shrillness of her insults, gathered around Albert and his ex-wife, who was sheltering her daughter Claudette from her horrid father.

Poor Albert! When he told me about the whole scene and his final failure, he had tears in his eyes. I felt sorry for him. I had left with him on this Pacific tour, from which our dear Christine had just come back to set up house with Robert, while I — whom everyone thought to be in Granby — was travelling in California with Albert. Then on our return — I mean, after what happened on 29th Ave. in San Francisco — Albert and I (never mentioning California or San Francisco) moved into an apartment on Nun's Island (on the eighth floor of the building beside the river). A few days after our return Albert came home and told me that Robert (my husband) had been hospitalized in critical condition with two bullets in his head. He was in coma.

You know what came after. Robert, Christine, Dr (Albert) Franconi, poor Suzanne etc. When he came back from Sacré-Coeur Hospital tonight, Albert went to sleep at once, and I watched another TV program. He did not speak to me, I suppose out of consideration. At once I went into his office, where I easily found the keys to the brown leather case I had bought for him in San Mateo. Christine's manuscript (she died as we know) was inside. I hadn't expected such a find. But now that I've read it I'll put it back in the case and her name will never again come up between Albert and myself. Never!

Signed: Suzanne B.-Franconi.
18 August 1969

The Antiphonary

Montreal, August 19, 1969

Dear love,

Since I discovered, when I got up, that my case had been unlocked and the manuscript replaced in a different way, I knew you had discovered everything, that you had read Christine's text and had made the obvious connections with the events of the last months. A few weeks of life together — that's no eternity! Far from it, you'll say, it's like a bad dream. Right after you came to live with me (after Robert had left you), you and I went to San Francisco. Christine had just come back from there, and three weeks later we were in Montreal again. Christine Forestier entered our lives two weeks later, at the moment of Jean-William Forestier's murder attempt. Christine has taken her life, Jean-William is dead as well. Robert is a survivor, but barely. I don't know why, but I have a strong feeling of having failed. I have behaved badly toward you, I almost frightened my two children, and I'll never see them again, though they were simply stolen from me. Our harmony has changed into a permanent discord (not openly, perhaps, but seriously just the same). Now that you know everything — apart from the wilder ravings of Christine, which I'm sure did not lead you astray — now that you have no illusions about the perfection of my love and my tendency to befoul everything I touch, I prefer to tell you openly that I'm ashamed of myself and intend to kill myself in my car.

It is precisely your intention to remain eternally faithful to a "sacred" love (ours) that lets me see how I have profaned the sacred bond between us. I can only conclude that I will never be worthy of it, and will never be able to bear my own unworthiness.

Don't hate me too much. And be sure that I love you, dark as my soul is; and I would so much have liked us to have a child. Things did not turn out that way. Perhaps this is better. I leave you (attached) a cheque for all my savings. I hope that

195

The Antiphonary

you will make use of this money to make a really fresh start in your life. I'm leaving before you awake. Farewell.

Albert

DATE DUE
DATE DE RETOUR

LOWE-MARTIN No. 1137·